Bernice and the Georgian Bay Gold

JESSICA OUTRAM

# Bernice and the Georgian Bay Gold

Second Story Press

**Library and Archives Canada Cataloguing in Publication**

Title: Bernice and the Georgian Bay gold / Jessica Outram.
Names: Outram, Jessica, author.
Identifiers: Canadiana (print) 20220474494 | Canadiana (ebook) 20220474559 | ISBN 9781772603187 (softcover) | ISBN 9781772603644 (hardcover) | ISBN 9781772603194 (EPUB)
Subjects: LCGFT: Novels.
Classification: LCC PS8629.U87 B47 2023 | DDC jC813/.6—dc23


Edited by Chandra Wohleber
Designed by Laura Atherton
Printed and bound in Canada

*Second Story Press gratefully acknowledges the support of the Ontario Arts Council and the Canada Council for the Arts for our publishing program. We acknowledge the financial support of the Government of Canada through the Canada Book Fund.*

Conseil des Arts du Canada | Canada Council for the Arts

Funded by the Government of Canada
Financé par le gouvernement du Canada

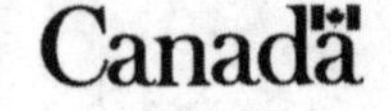


Published by
Second Story Press
20 Maud Street, Suite 401
Toronto, ON
M5V 2M5
www.secondstorypress.ca

*For my ancestors*

BYNG INLET
N
CLARK ISLAND
BIGWOOD ISLAND
SOUTH CHANNEL
INNER RANGE LT
OUTER RANGE LT
OLGA ISLAND
WHITEFISH
BURRITTS ISLAND
BURRITTS BAY
GERRY ISLAND
DANNY ISLAND
LIGHTHOUSE
GEREAUX ISLAND
DUFFY ISLAND
OLD TOWER ROCKS
MAGNETAWAN LEDGES
GEORGIAN BAY

*Summer 1914*

Gereaux Island Lighthouse
Byng Inlet, Georgian Bay
The traditional territory of the Anishinaabeg

# AUTHOR'S NOTE

Bernice's family speaks Michif French at home. The family describes their language at home as French. They describe traditional French Canadian as fancy French or Parisian French. Métis languages vary throughout the Métis Homeland. Each language can be looked at as having a varying degree, combination, or mixture of European and Indigenous languages and influences. For over a hundred years, Michif was a language passed on secretly between Métis parents and children. Bernice and her siblings were not allowed to speak Michif at school. By the next generation, her family would lose the language completely.

A special thank-you to the Métis Nation of Ontario, the Métis Languages Initiative team, and the Métis Languages Initiative Advisory members for adding Michif throughout this story.

"The translation was made possible through the MNO's Métis Languages Initiatives Advisory; we note that variations may occur based on the regional history of the language.

We have, in good faith, translated the following based on what we believe to be a true representation of the language within our region of Ontario."

# Part One

## *The Painted Canoe*

# 1

At sunset, I row into the bay to watch the sky change colors. Soft breezes circle the small rowboat, keeping the mosquitoes away. The water is flat and calm, so it's easy to float. A loon calls from Whitefish Channel. The sky turns from blue to gold to purple to orange. I feel small and big at the same time.

Our lighthouse stands on an island. All the colors of the sky reflect on the white shingles and red roof. Built to help ships on Georgian Bay find the Byng Inlet channel, it shines a big light from the tower across the water day and night. The light warns boats that they need to be careful because of the rocky shoreline and shoals.

Sunset is a special time to imagine stories in my head. West of the island is water as far as I can see. Other small islands rest nearby, mounds of rock that look like the backs of giant sleeping turtles. Can you imagine if one day the islands start to move like turtles waking up from a nap? I love to picture my bay turtles walking through the channels, so big their feet touch bottom in the deep water. They might even munch on a whole pine tree for a snack.

Today the Shebahonaning mountains look like shadows. Sometimes I hear them whisper, "We're waiting for you." I've always wanted to see them up close. Dad says *Shebahonaning* means "canoe passage." When Dad was a kid, he went to Shebahonaning once to visit our First Nation cousins, but the rest of us are always here at the lighthouse or in town, Byng Inlet North, mostly. I've never been anywhere else. What's across all that water?

Georgian Bay is big. I need to stay close to the islands; otherwise, Dad says I could get lost in the open water. How long would it take to row into the middle of Georgian Bay? Maybe if I had a giant bay turtle, I could travel on its back until I could see only water in every direction. Goose bumps rise on my arms and legs.

The giant ball of light sinks into the bay, and the sky looks on fire. I stand up in the boat and holler, "*Bawnn nui sawlèy!* Good night, sun!" Then I row home.

# 2

We live in the lighthouse on the island. My older brothers Ernest and William sit at the kitchen table playing cards. The light from an oil lamp flickers on their brown arms and hands.

"Go fish," Ernest says. His hair curls onto his forehead, bouncing in the shadows like a bug. He swats at his head, then realizes it's his hair. He tucks the curl so it stops moving.

"This game is for babies," William says. "Let's play something else, like euchre."

"It doesn't matter what we play. I'll win. I'm a winner." Ernest makes a face and dances in the chair, pointing at himself like a winner.

William rolls his eyes, grabs the deck of cards, and shuffles. "You're such a kid."

"And you'll lose, old man," Ernest, who's only nine, taunts.

William smiles. He likes being called old because he's twelve. "I am the man."

"You're both ridiculous." I take a card that had fallen onto the table, run across the kitchen, and put it on the window ledge across the room.

"Bernice!" shouts William.

"Grow up, Bea the Bean," Ernest says. Then he runs to grab the card.

My brothers laugh.

"Bea the Bean is no one to me." Once I have the last word, I leave before I have to hear another boring old joke. I hate it when they call me that nickname.

Mom and Dad sit in the living room. Dad snores in his chair, his blue fishing hat covering his face. Mom, cozy in her creamy nightdress, mends a pair of beige pants by the lantern.

Mémèr's already in bed. Sometimes I sit on the floor and listen to her talk in her sleep. It's fun to piece together what she's saying. A Mémèr "dream talk story puzzle." She's always sharing stories, even when she's sleeping. Mémèr says to pay attention to everything; nothing is an accident. Everything happens for a reason.

My oldest brother Alcide's fiddle softly plays. He's thirteen. At night he often sits at the top of the light tower on the turret, playing his fiddle to the bay. Dad says it's like a lullaby for the water.

"Good night, Bea," Mom says.

"Night," I reply.

It's easy to go to bed early tonight because my book is waiting for me. I'm nearly finished *Treasure Island* by Robert Louis Stevenson, and I need to see what happens next. I had a peek at the next chapter earlier today. Silver and his lieutenant are at the stockade waving a flag and saying they want a truce. I think for sure it's a trick.

# 3

In the morning, my eleven-year-old sister, Florence, shouts in my face, "Bea! How late did you read last night?"

My eyes slowly focus. She picks up the book from the floor, taps it on my head, and then puts it on the bed. She's already in her day dress, her long black hair braided.

"You fell asleep by the window again," she says. "Reading in the moonlight? Does that even work?"

"The book is so good! I think I finished it before I fell asleep." I pause. "I'll read the ending again just in case, because I don't remember what happened."

"Hey, Bea. There's a man sleeping in the living room. Did you hear him come in?" Florence asks.

"No! Why is there a man here?" I ask. "How come I didn't hear anything?"

"He's not even a cousin," she whispers. "*Yawrtonti kawm saw.* He arrived unannounced."

"Then who is he?" I run out to the ladder and look down to catch a peek. Our bedrooms are part of the lighthouse tower. Florence joins me on the landing. We squish together, squat, and try to see the downstairs without revealing ourselves.

At the beginning of *Treasure Island*, a mysterious visitor arrives at the inn, and everything changes for Jim Hawkins. Maybe this is our mysterious visitor, and everything will change starting today. Maybe my dream of having an adventure will come true. I gently tap a big toe on the wooden floor for good luck.

"No one but cousins sleep inside the house. This is strange," I whisper.

"Why isn't he outside in a tent?" Florence asks. "I asked Mom, and she just said to leave him alone, he's sleeping."

"When I came home last night from sunset, I didn't see anyone." I consider. "How could I have missed something as exciting as this?"

"Get dressed, and we can go downstairs and find out," Florence says. She drags me back to our room.

Most mornings everything is the same, but this morning a visitor in the living room is very different.

# 4

I quickly yank off my white nightdress and pull on my white day dress. Florence brushes and tugs at my thick hair until it's in two braids.

I must have read until late last night. Usually, I'm the first person to wake up. My brothers have even made their beds already. My bed is still made from yesterday. I guess that's what happens when I fall asleep by the window.

"Did you see what he looks like?" I ask.

"Not yet. He's covered by a sheet," she says.

"Do the boys know anything?"

"I'm not sure. They were up extra early this morning," she replies.

We scurry down the ladder to the main floor.

A man snores from the cot. Florence and I hold each other as we take a step closer. When he snorts in his sleep, we jump and run into the kitchen, giggling.

"Girls, you're going to wake our guest," Mom says. She lines up the ingredients for bannock on the counter. Flour, lard, salt, and baking powder.

"How can he still be sleeping?" I ask. "Who is that man?"

"You're one to talk, Bea. You just woke up," Florence teases.

Mom ignores us both. "Florence, please set up for the laundry."

"But, Mom, what about the man?" Florence whines.

"Enough questions. Florence, outside. Bea, have some breakfast, then you can help your sister." Mom's always cross in the morning. A mysterious visitor hasn't made her any cheerier.

Florence drags her bare feet across the floor, moving slower than a caterpillar. Eventually she makes it to the door and has no choice but to go outside to set up the water buckets and washboard. Florence always has so many chores to do. I can't imagine doing chores when there is a mystery as big as this to be solved.

When she's gone, I tiptoe back into the living room toward the cot for a closer look at his boots. They look like my brothers' boots, only they don't have as many scratches and marks. *Ya dé vra bèl bawt.* He has very nice boots.

The boys' boots smell so bad that Mom always asks them to keep them in the boathouse. No one wants to be around smelly boots. Why are these boots allowed inside? More strangeness.

Moving like a sneaky wolf, I return to the kitchen for answers to my questions. "Why are his boots inside?" I ask.

"Shh. Quiet, Bea," Mom replies. "Have some breakfast or go outside." She sprinkles salt into the bowl.

"Is he a tourist?" I ask.

"No." Mom kneads the dough with more force.

I slide to the living room for another look. The man's short brown hair pokes out the top of a white sheet, so white it glows.

I stand beside the cot. A bit of color shows through the sheet. He's wearing something red. Red is a fancy color. Who wears fancy red clothing to sleep?

Well, this is very mysterious. He is not a cousin or a tourist. He's not anyone we know from town either. *Yé ti étranj ou bin un étranjé? Ou bin lé deu?* Is he strange or a stranger? Or both? Focus, Bea, I tell myself. Now's not the time to play with words. There's a mystery to solve.

As I lean in to see his face, I trip on the man's boots and tumble to the floor with a thump.

The man jumps up from the cot, standing straight, looking at me. His face is red. He doesn't look happy. He's wearing red long johns.

Once I saw a woman in town wearing a long, silky red dress and white gloves. She wore a black hat that looked like a bird. I asked her who made her dress, and she said she didn't know. She bought it in a store. Mom makes all our dresses. They are always white, beige, or light blue. Did he buy his red long johns in a store? He must be rich to have red long johns.

In this moment, I can't help but wonder why the pirate Long John Silver is named after underwear. I giggle. Long John. Long johns.

The man looks confused. Maybe he doesn't realize he's inside our lighthouse.

"Where did you get red long johns?" I ask.

"Bernice Mary Normandin." Mom comes in from the kitchen. She stomps her foot and points to the door, handing me a bucket for fetching water. "Outside, now."

The man sits back on the cot. He still doesn't say anything. He rubs his eyes. Why doesn't he say good morning?

"Bernice. I'm not going to ask you again," Mom says. She marches toward me, her eyes like glowing coals.

I clutch the bucket and run outside faster than a rabbit into a bush.

# 5

Right away I notice a painted gray canoe resting on the rock by the boathouse. It must belong to the man. Why would anyone paint their canoe gray? Gray is the color of floors, not boats; boats are plain wood, not painted. Maybe a ship would be painted, but not a boat. All the floors in the lighthouse are painted the same gray as his canoe.

Who is he? Why is he here? First, last night he sleeps in our house. Second, he wears red long johns. Third, he has an ugly gray canoe.

"That's a Chestnut canoe," Dad says, walking over from the oil shed. "It's a newer boat. Not like the birchbark canoes, but it looks good and sturdy for these waters. I've heard good things about the Chestnut Canoe Company."

Every day Dad checks the oil in the light at the top of the tower. A few times a week, he goes to the oil shed, fills a five-gallon container with kerosene, and carries it up the tower to refill the light. Then he returns the empty container to the shed.

We also have two range lights on nearby islands that need filling a few times a week. It's my brothers' job to help with that.

Once in the spring and then again at the end of summer, a big boat stops by the island and refills our oil shed with enough kerosene for the house, the light, and the ranges. Keeping the light going is the most important thing. If it goes out, Dad will be fired. Boats will crash into the rocks. No one will know where the channel is to lead them into town.

"Who's that man in the kitchen?" I ask. Dad always tells me the truth.

"He said his name is Tom." Dad walks around the canoe, inspecting it from every angle.

"Is he lost?" I put the bucket down. Then I follow Dad, circling the canoe. When he leans in for a closer look, I lean in too.

"Look at those cedar ribs. This canoe doesn't look more than five years old," Dad says. He reaches to feel the smoothness of the boards in the belly of the boat. "Nothing like the birchbark canoes though."

"Do you know Tom?" I ask. It's best to continue asking Dad questions. Eventually he always answers.

He shrugs. "I met him yesterday." Dad winks. "Looks like you have a good mystery on your hands." Dad chuckles as he walks away toward the lighthouse.

Sometimes it feels like everyone keeps secrets from me on purpose.

"Yes!" Ernest shouts from over by the boathouse.

I walk toward him.

He's building a small birchbark canoe, using a big rock as his worktable. "This looks good, eh?" Ernest admires the frame of his toy canoe. "I did it without Dad's help this time."

Ernest started building canoes last summer. First, he helped Dad repair a canoe that had a leak. Then he asked if he could build a canoe. Ernest says he is curious about how things work, especially when it comes to boats. Dad says once Ernest masters building small canoes, he can try building a full-size one. The stitching on Ernest's last canoe wasn't tight enough and it sank. So, he is trying again.

"There's a strange man in the house. Who is he?"

"See, the birch is ready to fit around it next. Then I'm going to stitch it with white pine roots." Ernest smiles and carefully bends the birch around the frame.

"Did you even see the man in the house?" I ask.

"His canoe doesn't have any birchbark at all. I can't figure out how it stays together without the stitching," Ernest says.

"He wears red long johns!" I cry.

"Bea, why are you looking at a man's underwear?" Ernest laughs.

"Ew, I wasn't looking at his underwear! I may have woken him up by mistake," I reply.

"Well, he's not from around here. That's for sure." Ernest shifts his focus back to his project. "His gear's all in the boathouse. Did you check—?"

Before Ernest finishes his sentence, I'm already running to the boathouse.

# 6

All the best treasures are kept in the boathouse. Whenever we find anything like a lost peavey log roller or a beaver stick on the islands, we store it here. Mostly because Mom never lets us bring things into the lighthouse. William loves the log rollers. They're a straight bar of metal with a hook near the end. The lumbermen use them to pull logs. I love to collect beaver sticks. Dad says the beavers use their teeth to peel off the bark and layers of wood until the stick is smooth. Sometimes we use the bigger beaver sticks to hit rocks into the bay.

Inside the boathouse, there's a workbench for projects. Wooden docks line three walls with stacks of crates holding tools and parts. Dad's hammock hangs by the big doors to the water where the boats go in and out.

In the middle, over the water between the boats, hangs a swing Dad built for us for rainy days. It dangles from the huge rafters. We always climb up the beams too, almost like climbing a tree. They're so big, you can easily sit up there and relax. It's my favorite spot to read during the day, especially if it's too hot or too wet to read outside.

Piled in the corner on the left side I find Tom's *réginn dkamping*, his camping gear. There's a bundle that looks like a tent, but it's lighter than canvas. Next to it is a canvas bag with a pot, pan, and grill inside. A can of something with a strong smell, like Dad's turpentine. A crate with all sorts of strange things jammed inside: some rags, small squares of wood, brushes of different sizes, a bunch of little tubes with screw-on lids. I choose a tube and turn the lid.

A bright blue liquid is inside. I squeeze the tube a little and touch my finger on it.

"Bea!" Florence shouts.

I jump. The tube falls to the dock, and I nearly lose it through one of the bigger gaps.

"Why are you going through his things?" Florence scolds. "And what did you find?" She smiles.

"Not much, but this crate of stuff is kind of interesting," I say.

"What was that?"

"Something blue!"

Florence walks over for a closer look at the tube and the wet blue dot on my finger. "Looks like paint."

"Do you think all those tubes are paint?" I ask.

"Probably. William told me his name is Tom and he's from Toronto." Florence grabs the canvas bundle and takes it outside, placing it on the rock next to the canoe. "William also says he came in last night just before dark."

"William's the sneaky brother. Always knows everything. I wish I could move around like a fox like that." I wipe the blue from my finger onto the dock.

"William says the man's English." Florence laughs. "Mom told me you woke him up. You're in big trouble!"

"What's he doing here?" I ask.

Florence grunts as she carries the heavier canvas bag from the boathouse to the rocks by the canoe. "He's leaving soon. Too bad he can't stay. I told him I'd help him with his things. He's handsome, isn't he?" she asks.

"He's too skinny and he has a terrible sunburn," I reply.

"I'm going to ask him to sketch my portrait," she says as she drapes herself dramatically over his gear. "Maybe. If I work up the courage."

"So, he is an artist?" This explains all the things in the crate. We've had plenty of artists stop at the lighthouse over the years. They never sleep here though. Usually, they are going into town to paint portraits of the sawmill owners and their families. Our family has never had portraits painted. Why do you need a portrait of your family when you look at their faces every day? I see a portrait at school all the time of King George V. I don't like how his eyes follow me around the room.

"He's definitely an artist." Florence lowers her voice to speak like a man. "Hello, my name is Tom Handsome from Toronto. An artist."

"I'm Florence. Look at me." I imitate Florence's voice and drape myself on his gear next to her. "Paint my portrait so I can look at my own face every day."

"You're terrible!" Florence replies. "But if *he* has a sketch of me, I will always be with him. And then we fall in love, and he takes me to the city. I've always wanted to go to Toronto." She flutters her eyelashes and giggles.

"That's disgusting and perfect." I laugh.

"Mom asked me to get cedar for Tom to take on his journey. Do you want to come?" She starts toward the woods. "He needs it for tea."

"I'm going inside to hear him talk English." I skip to the lighthouse.

# 7

At the lighthouse door, I hear a murmur of voices.

I crouch so they can't see me. Through the screen I watch Dad and Tom hover over a piece of paper at the kitchen table.

"It's gold," Dad says in English. His eyes are serious, focused on the paper.

Dad speaks all the languages, like me. French, fancy French, English, some Ojibway. Wait, did he just say *gold*?

"Yes," Tom replies. "Thanks so much for your help. I can't thank you enough."

"You visited this spot yesterday?" Dad asks.

"Just after you found me nearly passed out in my boat," Tom explains. "If you hadn't come along when you did, I don't know if—"

"The sun and wind can be strong on the bay," Dad says. He reaches into the center of the table for his tobacco box and pipe. He begins to fill the pipe with tobacco. "Glad you navigated your way here by nightfall. You were determined to finish your quest for gold even though you were so sick from the sun."

Mom stands at the counter wrapping fresh bannock into one of our green holiday napkins.

"I've paddled since I was a kid and I've never had heatstroke like that." Tom puts his papers inside his bag. "I don't know what you did to make it go away, but I'm grateful. I'll need to be more careful. I still have a long way to go and much to do."

"We're not as young as we used to be." Dad winks, his leathery cheeks crinkling with his smile.

Mom passes Tom the bannock, and he tucks it into his bag.

"I'll never forget your kindness. You saved my life," Tom says to Dad. Tom's face is soft and smooth. He looks like he could cry, just like Alcide does sometimes when he's thankful.

Then Tom walks over to Mom and takes both her hands. "Thank you for the food. I haven't had a home-cooked meal in months."

Mom looks down at the floor, embarrassed by the attention. "*Marsi*," she says.

"*Merci*," Tom replies. His French sounds different from Mom's. "Your pickerel last night was the best I've ever had."

Mom must have cooked fish for Tom after bedtime! Please don't talk about food. I just want to hear more about that gold.

Dad notices me before I can move my ear from the screen. "Bea, what have I told you about spying?" Dad says in French.

I stand tall like a maple tree and make my eyes look all cute and innocent. "Hello, Mr. Tom. How do you do?" I say using my best English.

"Thanks for the wake-up this morning, Bea." Tom's eyes twinkle. His satchel drapes over his shoulder, buckled closed. Whatever they were looking at moments before is now sealed in that mysterious bag.

"I'm sorry, I tripped," I say. Then I curtsy the way Mom taught me. "Are you really an artist?"

"So they say." Tom laughs.

"What's in there?" I ask, pointing to his satchel. Maybe he even has some gold in his bag.

"That's enough questions for today, Bea," Mom says.

# 8

We make our way along the granite path to the Chestnut canoe. Dad helps load Tom's gear into the boat.

Florence runs from the bush clutching a handful of cedar. "I have the cedar," she shouts.

Dad slowly walks into the water to hold the canoe in place as Tom climbs inside. Dad's feet always know where the crevices are hidden. He secures his footing easily on the slippery rock. Whenever I try to find the crevices, my feet slide and I end up in the bay, soaked from head to toe.

"I didn't have time to bundle it." Florence passes Tom the cedar.

"Not a problem. Thanks for gathering it for me," he says. Tom smells the cedar and then tucks it into one of his packs.

"I don't know how often you drink cedar tea, so start with a small amount," Florence explains.

"Thank you." Tom smiles and waves.

Dad pushes the canoe away from the shore and joins us.

"Good-bye!" Tom shouts as he dips his paddle.

"*A prawchèn! Tsur vyindraw nourwèr.* Come back to see us, Tom Thomson," Dad shouts back.

As Tom paddles away from shore, I run through the kitchen and up the steps to the top of the light tower. Standing outside on the turret, leaning over the rail, I watch as Tom paddles north until the Chestnut canoe is a speck among the islands. Then Tom disappears.

# 9

In the living room, all that's left behind is the empty cot and the white sheet. Mémèr rocks in her chair by the window.

"Who was here? What did I miss?" Mémèr asks.

"Did you meet Tom?"

"Who's Tom?" she asks.

"An artist, from Toronto. He slept here last night. In red long johns!" I explain.

"Did he forget something?" Mémèr passes me a piece of paper.

On one side it has some letters. I can't read the words, but I know that they are definitely words. The words are beside shapes, almost circles, with lines connecting them.

"What is it?" I ask.

"Looks like a secret." Mémèr smiles.

On the other side of the paper is a sketch of an island, but it looks different from ours. There's more bush, and the trees are closer to the water. Our bush is more inland. This doesn't look like a portrait of a person or a family at all.

And then I realize what it is: a map to the place with the gold that Dad and Tom were talking about! *Mon awr.* My gold. A mysterious stranger visited us, and now I have a treasure map, just like in *Treasure Island.* It's official. I have an adventure.

"Can I keep this?" I ask.

"If you wish." Mémèr closes her eyes for a morning nap.

Folding it carefully first, I put the map in the pocket of my dress and then run out to my spot on the island so I can study it more closely without anyone bothering me.

# Part Two

## *Mémèr and the Ancestors*

# 10

The wind howls before sunrise. I lie awake in bed. Under the mattress I feel for the map. It's still there. So far, my family has no idea that I have a treasure map. They always keep so many secrets. Finally, I have one of my own. I'll show them I'm not Bea the Bean anymore. I'm eight years old. I can have my own adventures. I look around the bedroom in the dark. Florence and my brothers are still sleeping. Excellent. This gives me more time for making plans.

What does real gold even look like? In *Treasure Island*, they find barrels of gold coins. Could there be an island near our lighthouse with barrels of gold?

So far in my life I have seen pennies, nickels, and dimes. We don't see coins too often. Mom and Dad have a jar of them hidden in their room. William and Alcide earn coins at the coal docks. Twenty cents an hour. Or is it ten cents an hour? I never pay much attention. I wish I could get coins too.

The coal arrives in a gigantic ship that passes by the lighthouse on its way to the coal docks. Then Alcide and William row to town for a few days to work. Alcide and William help to dump coal from the ship into an open hopper car that travels on the tramway tracks to the big rail yard. I'm not sure how they help move the coal, but I do know they are covered in coal, black from head to toe, when they come home.

When the men from the city arrive by train to go out to the fishing camps on Tourist Day, they throw coins at the children in the rail yard. Dad always picks up a few fishermen at the station to lead them by boat to their fishing camps in the bay. Ernest and I go with him, but Dad never lets us pick up the coins. All I want is a soda at Cornish's Store, and Dad will say, "Let's go, Bea. We have all we need. *Sé tout pour tsusuit.* That's all for now."

Why haven't Dad and Mom talked about gold on these islands before? If we had that gold, maybe I could buy some fabric for a new dress. Or a train ticket to Toronto. Alcide told me they have motor cars in the city. I can't even imagine going anywhere any other way than by boat or dogsled. I wonder if a motor car can go fast. I love to go fast.

It would be such a good story if I found gold on an island. Then, in a hundred years, when I'm as old as Mémèr, I'll sit in the rocking chair and tell all the children about my adventures.

Mémèr's the oldest of everyone. She's Dad's maamaa. Her given name is Christina Scholastique Berger, and she's lived at the lighthouse on this island since it was built, even before Dad was born. Dad was born in the lighthouse, and we were all born here too.

Maybe I'll be the next lighthouse keeper. That would make William so mad. He says he's going to be the next keeper. I want to be the first girl lighthouse keeper. Ha! Heads would spin! Or maybe I'll be a writer like Robert Louis Stevenson and share stories for kids. At school, Miss Gallagher told me that Robert Louis Stevenson's dad was a lighthouse engineer who designed lighthouses. When she told me that, I started drawing pictures of lighthouses all the time, but they always ended up looking like our lighthouse. I'm better at stories than drawing. When I finish school, I'm not doing chores like Florence. I have big plans, and these plans need a big adventure.

Two years ago, when I was six, Pépèr died. Pépèr taught me all about how to watch for a good story. He always said to gather the stories I find and tell them over and over in my head, to print them on my mind so I can share them with the next generation. He said that to find stories, I needed to find adventures too.

Pépèr said, "No one can ever take your stories, Bea. They are always yours."

## 11

Yesterday, Mémèr rocked in her chair as she beaded a blueberry design. She beads on deer hide for summer boaters who visit the lighthouse. Usually, it's a small piece with a flower that she adds a pin to on the back. Other times she beads on moccasins or a small bag. Sometimes she even beads on a tablecloth or a man's vest.

When Mémèr places beautiful *garnitsur*, beadwork, on the kitchen table, boaters often request to buy it.

"One day, I'll make you a special flower," she tells me.

I really want to learn how to bead. Florence is already beading moccasins. It isn't fair that Florence always gets to do everything first. And she is so perfect too. Not only is she the best baker in the family, but Florence also creates the most beautiful bead designs and embroidery. She adds little flowers to everything. She even embroiders flowers and plants on our dresses. Florence put a little blueberry plant on the sleeve of my dress and a daisy on the sleeve of hers.

"I have much to teach you, *ma pchi*," Mémèr says, using her nickname for me: "my little." Then she reaches out and takes both my hands in hers. Her hands are always soft and smooth. I lean in close to smell the soap on her skin.

"First lesson: don't talk so much." She puts her hand up to my lips. "*Taw unn bouch, deu zieu, pi deu awrèy.* You have one mouth, two eyes, and two ears. Watch and listen more than you speak. Otherwise, you're going to miss something important."

Pépèr taught me the best way to find stories is to watch for them, to pay attention. Pépèr would have loved to have known about my treasure map. Pépèr told me it's important to follow questions. "Questions are like stars," he'd say. "Pick one and see where it leads."

Where does this map lead? Should I take the canoe or the rowboat to get there? What does one pack for an adventure? Has Mémèr seen gold? She's lived here so many years. She knows everything.

She's the only one who knows about the map so far. I have so many questions to ask her as soon as she wakes up.

Mémèr will help me follow these questions. I just know it. Questions lead to adventures. Adventures turn into stories. It's all planned.

I look out the window into the dark sky. Why is sunrise late today? Or am I too early? The wind whistles, and thunder rumbles in the distance. Big waves smash into the shore. Whenever it storms, we're stuck on the island.

After breakfast, I decide to check on Mémèr. How can she still be sleeping in this storm? The ladder to the second floor is too steep for Mémèr to climb, so she has a small bedroom on the first floor. The rest of the family sleeps upstairs: Mom and Dad in the small room and all the kids together in the big one.

I creak open Mémèr's door and tiptoe two steps into the dark. Rain patters at the window. She snores gently under the quilt Mom made her long ago. Wait. Something's on Mémèr's head. *Ke sé kis pas?* What's happening? *Sé ptsi kawm unn souri avèk dla fourur.* It's small and furry, like a mouse. *Aw non, stunn souri!* Oh no, it *is* a mouse!

"Oh! Mémèr, wake up! There's a mouse!" I cry. The mouse runs from Mémèr's head down to her feet, jumps from the bed, across the floor, and disappears into a crack in the plaster wall.

Mémèr's eyes pop open. She feels her head. "Who was here? What did I miss?" she says.

"A mouse! A mouse!" I cry, jumping up and down, squealing.

"A mouse?" she asks.

"There was a mouse sitting on your head!" I reply.

"Did you ask it why it was there?" Mémèr asks.

"No! Why would a mouse be on your head?"

"Good question," she says. "Let's ask Pépèr."

"But he died," I explain.

"Who died?" she asks.

"Pépèr."

"When? I was just talking to him."

I want to cry. "Pépèr died. Two years ago."

"Oh. Then who was here?" she asks.

"A mouse," I reply.

"Oh, is that all, *ma pchi*," she says. "Probably just looking for breakfast. Don't worry. I'm fine. Let's go out."

I help Mémèr to stand up from the bed and hold her arm as we walk out the side door and down the steps to the outhouse.

Rattlers, bears, and spiders are all just fine with me, but mice in the house are totally frightening. I never imagined a mouse sitting on someone's head. How will I ever sleep again?

"It caught me by surprise," I whisper.

"Mice have a way of doing that," she says. Mémèr's fingers quickly run across the top of my hair. They send goose bumps and shivers through me. She smiles. "They're just mice, that's all." She does it again and again until I giggle. We laugh all the way to the outhouse.

When she's finished, Mémèr shouts, "Okay."

We walk back to the lighthouse together arm in arm. Strong winds nearly blow her over. Her long hair flies wildly in all directions. The rain soaks us through our clothes.

"Too much wind today to row," she says.

"But I want to go somewhere," I whine.

"Not today, *ma pchi*," she says. "Do you remember our name for the bay?"

"*Waaseyaagami-wiikwed.* Shining Waters Bay."

"Where are those shining waters today?" She pats my arm. "They always come back. And eventually the wind will calm too."

On a sunny day the bay sparkles and shines. On a cloudy day the water's dark, almost black. "*Chtèm Mémèr.* I love you, Mémèr." I squeeze her hand.

"This will pass," she says. Then she sings, "*En roulant ma boule en roulant, en roulant ma boul-ou-le....*" Pépèr sang this as he paddled on long journeys as a voyageur in a big canoe during the fur trade. I know the English words too. *On and on my ball rolls on, on and on my ball.* It repeats over and over. We sing it every day.

After we change into dry clothes, I help Mémèr into her rocking chair in the living room. The cot's gone, and there's no trace that Tom was ever here. William lies on his belly by the window playing solitaire. I'll need to wait to ask Mémèr about the map.

# 12

In the afternoon, once everyone's finally busy and we're alone, I sit on the floor at Mémèr's feet. She sits in her rocking chair. I can't wait any longer.

"Mémèr, can you keep a secret?" I ask.

"Of course not," she says. "But I can forget a secret."

"I have some questions."

"Who was here? What did I miss?" she asks.

"You know Tom," I whisper. "The one in the painted canoe."

"Never met him," she says.

"You gave me a piece of paper that he left behind," I remind her.

"Is this where you saw a mouse?"

"No, Mémèr, the mouse was on your head when you were sleeping!" I reply.

"Oh, if he was sleeping near the kitchen, it would make more sense for the mouse to be on *his* head." She laughs.

"I'm serious. This is important." I lean toward her and take her hand. "It's huge."

"I'm listening, *ma pchi.*" She closes her eyes. "My ears work better if my eyes rest."

"Dad and Tom were talking about gold. I think it's a treasure map." I explain.

"Now I remember Louis and Cecilia telling me about some gold," she says, using my parents' first names.

"What did they tell you? I must know everything."

"Now that my eyes are resting, the mouth wants to rest too." Mémèr makes sleeping noises. Then I feel her fingers running over the top of my head.

"Mémèr!" I cry.

"It's that mousey coming back to snack on your hair." Her eyes twinkle as she smiles.

That night after dinner, Mémèr says, "Let's go out."

She holds on to my arm as we walk. The sun's melting from sky to water.

"See, it's calm now. Everything is quiet," she says. "Can you hear them?"

"Hear who? It's just us, Mémèr."

"Come with me." She leads me down a different path, past the outhouse. It takes us to the northwest side of the island. "One minute, I need to sit." Mémèr sits on a big rock, placed in just the right spot for a view of the bay.

"I haven't been to this rock before."

"I know. You shared a secret with me. I will share a secret

with you. Reciprocity. That's how giving and receiving work," she explains.

"Is it about the gold?" I ask.

"Sit on this rock with me." She taps the rock beside her.

I sit next to Mémèr. She wraps an arm around me and squishes.

"Close your eyes," she whispers. "Listen. What do you hear?"

"Waves. Wind. Leaves rustling."

"Yes. And what else?" she asks.

"My heartbeat?"

"Yes, and...?"

"Your voice?"

"Listen better, *ma pchi*. Pay attention. Stretch your ears across the shining waters." She squeezes me closer.

"Whispers?" I ask.

"Yes, and?"

"I don't know."

"Listen with both ears," she says.

Then in a whoosh all at once I think I hear Pépèr singing. "Do I hear Pépèr?" I ask.

"Yes, *ma pchi*. Listen. Listen closely and you can hear your ancestors. Hear all your relations. The water and wind, the insects and animals. And once in a while, in the stillness by the water, the voices of our family. They whisper to us in our hearts. Usually, we are too busy or too noisy to hear them."

The bay settles as the sun disappears. After Mémèr teaches me how to listen for the ancestors, I feel like I'm in the middle of a story with them. Maybe this is what Pépèr meant when he talked about stories finding me. These voices may have some stories to share if I listen closely enough.

We sit quietly awhile by the water together to listen for the voices of our ancestors. I wait until Mémèr is ready to chat again, in the meantime praying that the ancestors will help guide me on my adventure to find the gold. They were voyageurs for generations. The voyageurs paddled in large birchbark canoes from Montreal to Mackinac and much further than that too. Each canoe was filled with goods they used to trade for furs. We have adventure in our blood.

Mémèr breaks the silence. "This week Mémèr will teach you beading. My maamaa taught me when I was a *pchi* like you. Back when we lived in Waubaushene."

"That's a nice name for a place: Waubaushene. The sounds make me smile when I say it. When I say Byng Inlet, I don't smile. It doesn't have the right sound for a smile."

"Our town, Byng Inlet, was named after a British naval officer, Admiral John Byng," Mémèr says. "Well, I guess it's called Dunlop now, after an engineer at the rail station. But we all still call it Byng Inlet North."

"Why do they name places after men?" I ask.

"In the old days, places had different names that described their spirits, like Shining Waters Bay. So much has changed since the War of 1812."

"Like what?"

"When Maamaa had to move to Penetanguishene, she lost a lot. Each generation we lose a little more of the ways of our community. It started with the names of places. People like to name places after what's important to them. As more people from overseas came to our lands and waters, they decided to change many of the names."

I walk over to the edge of the shore. "And your maamaa's out there with Pépèr now?" I point to the bay.

Mémèr nods. "Maamaa was the daughter of Chief Buffalo, Kechewaishke. Loon Clan. He was a great Ojibway leader. She only met him a couple of times though. He moved around so much, so she was raised by her maamaa and the community."

"Well, who was her maamaa?" I ask.

"A Saulteaux named Isadore," she answers.

"What is Saulteaux?"

"People of the Rapids," Mémèr smiles.

"I love the rapids!" I exclaim. "There are amazing rapids down the Magnetawan River too."

"Maamaa was born on Mackinac Island. After the War of 1812, the British soldiers asked our kin to move to Potagannissing, now called Drummond Island. What was once a big place, Turtle Island, was becoming two countries. The United States and Canada. As the maps were drawn, the British told our kin to move one more time to Penetanguishene in 1828."

"That's a lot of places and names, Mémèr. It's confusing."

"Maamaa's story is complicated. Mine is simple. I've spent my whole life on this Shining Waters Bay. First, in Waubaushene and then here." Mémèr joins me by the water. She pulls dried tobacco leaves from her dress pocket.

Mom and Dad grow a couple of tobacco plants on the island, so Dad always has some for his pipe and Mémèr always has some for her prayers. She sprinkles the small pieces of tobacco leaves into the bay to offer thanks. "We send our ancestors thanks. So many cousins lost everything. Homes. Horses and goats. Furniture. Land. There were dark days for many years," she explains.

"It makes me want to cry," I whisper.

"Me too." Mémèr puts her arm around me. "But one day in all this darkness Maamaa met Joseph Berger: a strong, handsome French voyageur, another Drummond Islander. They got married in Penetanguishene at St. Anne's and lived in Waubaushene, where I was born. And then I met a strong, handsome son of a Métis voyageur, another Drummond Islander, your Pépèr. And one day you will marry a great adventurer too."

"Not me! Instead of marrying an adventurer, I'm going to be one. Mémèr, do you ever want to go back to Waubaushene to visit?" I ask.

"Home is here now, on this island, *ma pchi.*" She takes a deep breath.

"How old are you? Are you a hundred?" I ask.

Mémèr's eyes, bright like lightning bolts, look at me a moment. "A hundred?!" she cries. "That's enough story for today."

# 13

"Say good-bye to the ancestors. It will be dark quickly. We'll come back another day." Mémèr starts on the path back to the lighthouse.

*Good-bye, Pépèr*, my heart whispers. *I will listen for you.*

When we are nearly to the lighthouse, Mémèr stops.

"Pépèr always said you are a story keeper, Bernice. This is why I share all this with you, to help share Pépèr's lessons. You are now the story keeper for our family. And one day you will pass this honor to someone who will be story keeper when you are gone." Mémèr looks into my eyes. "Collect all the stories you can, Bernice."

I think I hear Pépèr whisper, "Start with the gold." He must know about the treasure.

"I'll find it," I whisper toward the water.

We walk by the pen where our huskies, Whiskey and Wine, spend most of their time. They run over to the fence to see me.

"I'm going to name the island with the gold after you," I tell them.

That night I can't sleep. I feel my ancestors around me. It's like they followed me home from the bay to the lighthouse. I imagine Pépèr reading my *Treasure Island* book by the window. Great-Mémèr and Great-Pépèr are studying my treasure map, arguing about which direction to go to find the island with the gold. Is it the north shore or the south shore? There are others wandering around our room too. People I've never met. I sit up in bed in the dark and watch the room fill up with cousins, aunties, uncles, and generations of family.

One by one they join in the excitement of my adventure, offering advice. Take the canoe, not the rowboat. Pack some food. Bring Ernest. No, bring Florence. Bring both. Bring Ernest. We can't decide. Start tomorrow. Wait a week. You'll need tools. Ask your dad. No, ask William. It's not about the gold. Or is it? Watch for bears. No, watch for snakes. Wait for Crow to return. Yes, the gold will wait too.

All the while, my brothers and my sister snore, sleeping through all of it.

# Part Three

## *Captain Rickley*

# 14

We have already rowed halfway down the Magnetawan River toward town when Ernest realizes he forgot his shoes. I don't care though. Nothing can ruin my adventure. It all starts today with a trip to town. I'm going to find someone there who can teach me about gold and how to read this map. It feels like my whole body is lit up with fire.

"How did you forget your shoes again?" Florence asks. She nudges Ernest into the side of the boat. They share a bench in the stern.

Ernest shoves her back.

Alcide dips the oars in the water and then slices the air before dipping them again. "We're not turning back now," he says.

"Maybe there's a pair in the house at the Point?" Florence offers.

"Can we stop by Eddie's? Maybe he has an extra pair?" Ernest asks. He leans on Florence and stretches his bare feet out over the side of the boat. Eddie is Ernest's best friend and fishing pal. He lives in town. Ernest is always looking for an excuse to visit.

While he rows, Alcide swiftly pushes Ernest's feet back into the boat without missing a beat.

"Bea and I will take you," Florence volunteers.

"That's because you have a crush on Eddie," Ernest teases.

"Florence has a crush on everyone!" I laugh.

Florence laughs too.

"Looks like you have a plan," Alcide says.

We pass the Clarke, White and Company Sawmill, the first of four sawmills on the river. Dad says this is one of the biggest lumber towns in all of Canada. Do we have enough trees for all that? Sounds like a big responsibility to me. That's the sawmill company that built the first lighthouse on a tiny island next to Gereaux Island. Dad says it was unsafe in the winds. The government built another one on the bigger island, our island, that was safer a couple years later in 1873, and that's the one we live in.

I don't think men at the mills can help me with my map. I need to find someone who knows the waters, like a fisherman or a guide. Someone who knows the kind of stuff Dad knows. This would all be so much easier if I just asked Dad, but he'll either want to join me or say no. For once, I want my own adventure. I want to show them I'm not a baby anymore.

"If the clocks hadn't stopped again," Ernest says, "maybe I would've remembered shoes."

"You never wear shoes," I say. "Fat chance."

"In my defense, it's very hot." Ernest pouts.

"The bigger question is, how late are we today?" Alcide asks. "I don't want to lose any wages at the coal docks."

"I have no idea what time it is," Florence adds.

"Dad said it was still morning!" I shout. The sun's high now, and the skies are clear blue.

"Dad has no idea about time," William says. "He makes stuff up."

"He said the angle of the sun told him," I continue. "And the dew."

"Last time this happened, it was lunchtime when we got to town," Alcide says. "Clocks aren't his thing. Dad has other skills. Like fishing."

"Or healing," I add.

"Kiss the ring of the seventh son of a seventh son," Ernest says. He reaches his hand outside the boat toward a mallard swimming nearby.

"Seems like something out of one of your books, Bea," Florence says.

"Mémèr says it's very serious. I laughed once, and she told me it was bad luck to laugh at someone's gifts," I explain.

"Ernest, you're more like the third son of a seventh son of a seventh son," William suggests. The mallard quacks.

"I agree, you shouldn't joke about that stuff. Last month a guy came to the island from Byng Inlet. He had so much pain, he could barely move. After he met with Dad, he walked no problem," Alcide says.

"How do you explain that?" Florence asked.

"It's a mystery," William answers.

Florence waves across the river to people on the shore at the big sawmill in Byng Inlet. "Maybe it's still morning?" A jam of logs lines the riverside, ready to be pulled to land and run through the mill.

"Whatever time it is, I'm going to find a snack first," Alcide says.

"I'll head over to the coal docks," William says.

"It always takes so long to get to town," Ernest says. "Why can't they make faster boats?"

"Or shorter rivers!" Florence adds.

"Hey! You have it easy, just relaxing like tourists for the last two hours," Alcide says. "I've done all the rowing!"

We park at the Point, where the Still River meets the Magnetawan River. Our old wooden two-story winter house looks sad. Lonely or something. We never stay here in the summer, except for the odd night when we come to town. It's smaller than the lighthouse. The swimming and fishing aren't as good as out in the bay. Also, Dad prefers the whole family to be with him. He doesn't like to be alone.

When I step inside the house, it smells like sage and cedar. Mom puts dried leaves and branches around the house, usually near the doors and windows. The cedar branches hang from nails in the wall. The sage sits on ledges or in small bowls in each room. Sometimes we collect sweetgrass too. Mom says it helps our house have good energy, especially when we are not here in the summer. In the winter she says our songs and stories and Florence's baking fill the house with good energy.

As I walk through the kitchen to the living room, a whoosh of stories from Mémèr and Pépèr wash over me. The house was built by the government as a winter home for the lightkeeper when Dad was a kid.

Pépèr retired from being a lightkeeper in 1901, and then they had nowhere to live. The government told them to leave, giving the house to Dad. That's one reason Mémèr and Pépèr moved in with us. They had no money and no home. Mom often talks about how much things have changed and that we need money or land. After I learned to read, Dad showed me the letter he got when he became lighthouse keeper. He keeps the letter in a special cedar box on a shelf in the living room.

When I find gold, I'll buy Mom and Dad a new house, so they don't have to live in government houses or on government land anymore. I've never met the government and don't know much about them, but Dad says they can cause a lot of problems for us if we don't do what they say.

"It feels so empty," Florence says.

"I hate staying here in the summer," Ernest adds.

"Hopefully we can get some work today and tomorrow," William says. "See you later!" He lets the screen door slap behind him as he runs outside.

Alcide opens each of the cupboards one by one. "I just need to find something to eat, then I'll come and join you at the docks, Willy."

"He didn't hear you. Already gone." I pull a scone from my pocket and pass it to Alcide. This morning I tucked an extra in each pocket just in case I was hungry later.

"Thanks, Bea." Alcide takes the scone with one hand and ruffles my hair with the other. Then he runs out of the house after William.

"Let's go to Cornish's Store to pick up the things from Mom's list," Florence offers.

"Let's go to Eddie's first," Ernest says. "No shoes here. Just winter boots."

"I always like visiting Eddie. Or wear those boots," Florence says.

"What if I go to town without shoes?"

"Mom says you need to wear shoes in town. If you don't, she'll find out. She always finds out. And then what?" Florence asks.

"Hmmm…more chores. No fishing with Eddie. Fine. I'll wear the hot big boots for now," Ernest says.

"Let's go to the spur line yard," I suggest. Maybe then we can loop by the docks to find someone to help me. I can't wait to start my search for gold.

First, what does this map mean? Who will be able to read it? How do I sneak away without Ernest and Florence noticing? I'll just need to wait for the perfect moment to disappear.

We head out toward the swing bridge.

# 15

The spur line yard looks deserted. Spur lines are short tracks that branch off from the main rail track so that small railcars can move the coal from the docks to the rail yard.

The main rail yard is about a 40-minute walk along the Still River from here. The steam locomotive first came to town when I was two years old. Mom and Dad took us to see it that day, but I don't remember. Now we only get to see the rail yard a few times a year. It has so many little houses. Dad showed them all to us: oil house, hose house, hydrant house, power house, outhouse. Everything has its own little wooden house. I love the seven bunkhouses made of unused boxcars lined up in a row. What would it be like to live in a train car?

But the spur line yard is boring. Just little tracks and one shack. I thought we might find some workers at least. Where is everyone?

We walk to the shack to see if someone's inside.

"Empty." Ernest looks in the door. Then he checks the outhouse. "Empty."

"Maybe we should just go to town, get the stuff for Mom?" I offer. I need a new plan to find someone because no one is here. It might be better to go directly to town. Then I can sneak away while Florence and Ernest are distracted in the store.

"Let's look around back," Florence says.

Ernest runs to check the other way by a small grouping of shingled houses where some of the workers live.

"No one here either," he shouts.

"Feels like a ghost village," Ernest says.

"Usually we meet the most interesting people," I reply. "Did something happen?"

We hear his squeaky voice first. "Everyone's gone," a voice hollers in English.

"Over here," Florence shouts.

Ernest and I sprint to them.

A boy a bit older than us wearing suspenders sits on a hand cart on the track, whittling.

"What are you doing?" Florence asks. We're used to quickly switching to English when we're in town.

"You can't really ride on that, can you?" Ernest asks.

"I can do whatever I want." He folds his knife and puts it in his pocket.

"That doesn't even look safe," I challenge.

"Big deal," he replies. His face is round, and he wears a blue and white striped rail hat with the peak flipped up.

"Where are all the people?" I ask.

"Did something happen?" Florence asks.

"Let me check." He jumps out of the hand cart and looks around in an exaggerated way. He puts his right hand over his brow like a salute as his body slowly twists around the area. "All the people are not here. I'm Albert."

I roll my eyes. "We can see no one is here. *Where* is everyone?" I repeat.

"Ernest, Bea, and Florence." Ernest introduces us. Then he looks at me, telling me to be quiet with his eyes.

"Did everyone leave you here—*alone*?" I ask. Since he was being so difficult, I wanted to be difficult too.

"What do you want, kids?" Albert asks. He takes a couple of steps toward us, then fixes his eyes on Florence.

"Who are you calling kids?" Ernest replies. He steps in front of Florence. The two boys stare at each other, standing about a foot apart. Albert's nearly twice the size of Ernest, who is scrawny. Town kids can be unpredictable. It's hard to know what they're thinking.

I watch Ernest clenching his fists.

"I keep the tracks clear. Watch over the place." Albert steps back and smiles. "Don't worry. I'm one of the good guys." He winks.

Ernest relaxes his hands. "Good to know," he says. I can tell that Ernest doesn't trust this guy.

"Our clocks stopped, and it would be helpful to know the time." Florence smiles. She always does this when my brothers fight. She finds a way to get them to focus on something else. It's true that our clocks stopped, but it doesn't matter about time. I need to find someone to help me with this map.

"There was an accident this morning at the mill, Holland and Emery, and all the guys from the spur line yard went over to help out," Albert explains. He puffs out his chest.

"Another fire?" I remember how scary it was when one of the Graves Bigwood mills burned down last year.

"Not this time," Albert says. He leans on the hand cart. It starts to roll. He readjusts so his foot rests on it. When I giggle, Florence elbows me in the stomach.

"Did another guy get sliced by the saw?" Ernest asks.

"From what I heard a boy fell from the tramway. He slipped and then went twenty feet down into the Magnetawan River. Someone said he hit his head on a floating log and drowned."

"That's horrible," Ernest says.

I think about my brothers working at the coal docks and hope it isn't as dangerous there. If I find gold, maybe my brothers won't have to work. And then maybe Florence wouldn't have to start thinking about getting married, flirting with boys all the time.

Florence finished Grade 6 a couple months ago, the highest grade we have in town. She really wants to be a teacher, but Dad said we can't afford for her to have the training classes. When Florence asked her teacher Miss Gallagher about it, she said it's $50 to buy just a uniform for the teacher-training school, which is run by nuns, and then a three-hour train trip to North Bay, where the school is located. Don't they have closer schools? Or other schools without nuns?

I wish we had more choices. The gold could change everything for us.

Albert reveals a pocket watch with cracked glass attached to his belt by a string. "It's one o'clock." He winks at Florence.

"Thank you." Florence smiles.

I groan.

"Did you hear there could be a war soon?" Albert asks.

"What kind of war?" I ask.

"I don't know. My boss says an Archduke of Austria was

murdered in Bosnia. The guys told me the other day that the British are going to fight, and then we'll help the British. My dad will be a soldier, for sure," he explains.

"That doesn't make sense. A war? There must be more to the story than that," Ernest says.

Suddenly a giant man steps out of the bush from the other side of the tracks.

"Run!" Albert says. "That's Captain Rickley."

# 16

Florence grabs my arm and pulls me with her as she follows Ernest who follows Albert as we dash away.

"Hey, kids!" Captain Rickley yells in the deepest voice I've ever heard. "Wait!"

We run as fast as we can, jumping over small bushes and rocks, crouching under leafy branches, and sliding across slippery patches of moss until we make it to the bridge to Little Italy.

"We should be safe here," Albert pants. "If he really wanted our attention, we'd still hear him hollering. Sometimes we can hear him yelling all the way from Key Harbour."

"Are we okay?" I ask. My heart thumps and sweat drips from my face, arms, and knees.

"Have you heard the stories?" Albert pants as he speaks. "He boils up rattlesnake meat in soup!"

"And?" I ask. "Our dad ate rattler meat before too. Plus, there's no way you can hear all the way from Key Harbour."

Albert cautiously scans the area, paying close attention to the direction we came from when we first saw Captain Rickley.

"He's famous. At school, I heard he caught a sturgeon that was nearly ten feet long," Florence says.

"Eddie told me it took three fish boxes to carry it!" Ernest continues.

"Well, I've heard that if you look him in the glass eye, you'll be cursed," Albert says. "Some even say he is a ghost from the wreck of the *Northern Belle* steamer that sunk up the river sixteen years ago."

"But everyone survived," Florence says. "They got into a lifeboat before the *Belle* went down in flames. Our dad helped Captain Jacques. He told us all about it. Dad even took us swimming there to see the wreck. On a clear day you can see shadows along the bottom of the river. It was so mysterious, like it was haunted or something. I didn't know that underwater could have that strangeness to it."

"He fishes near Dead Island," Albert whispers. "That's mysterious *and* strange."

"If he stays off the island, it's fine," Ernest explains. "We've fished near there before too."

Albert whispers, "*And* I heard he's friends with the people who live over by Sand Bay."

"You mean our—" I start.

Ernest hits me before I can say the word "cousins." We have cousins everywhere.

"We better go to town," I offer. Albert is annoying. Maybe I can find Captain Rickley. He would be able to help me read the treasure map. I just know it. Captain Smollett in *Treasure Island* was very knowledgeable and trustworthy.

"Eddie's house is just down this path. Let's go see if he's

home. I've had enough of these hot boots. Nice to meet you, Albert." Ernest nods politely but without his usual smile. Then he walks down the path to Eddie's.

Florence follows. "Come on, Bea."

"I better get back to work then," Albert says. "Until we meet again, sweet Florence. Keep an eye out for news about that war! And beware of Captain Rickley!" Albert bows like a gentleman and returns down the path back to the spur lines.

This is my chance to escape and go to town before the others get there. Then I will find Captain Rickley again. Since he's a captain, he will understand maps. Maybe he will know about the gold too since he grew up on the islands just like Dad. I'm not afraid of him.

"I'm going straight to town to see if Delia is home," I share. Delia's my best friend from school, and I often visit her when we come to town. They won't suspect anything. "You can meet me at the store."

"Okay!" Ernest says.

"We won't be long," Florence says.

They cross the bridge to Little Italy where Eddie lives. Mom says when the mills opened, Eddie's family moved all the way from Italy with some other families, so everyone calls their island Little Italy. I've been to their island plenty of times. It's a great place to play hide and seek.

Now, I have a mission. I walk along on the path toward town, then turn right and move through the woods toward the swing bridge. I won't be visiting Delia today. I'm going to find Captain Rickley.

I follow Albert like a trapper, stepping gently, toe to heel like Dad taught me. This way the sound from my feet goes behind me, instead of toward him. Each step is slow, light, and gentle. I even pay attention to keep my breath quiet. It isn't easy to stay hidden behind trees because he nervously scans the woods in all directions, even the ground.

Is he afraid of snakes too? Sometimes he hears a twig snap. He doesn't know it's me accidentally stepping on twigs as I try to move around branches that poke near my face. He freezes, puts out his hands to either side like he's balancing in a boat on the waves. Maybe he holds his breath too. I don't really know why the woods scare him or why he's so worried about Captain Rickley.

In *Treasure Island*, there were some characters who were meant to be scary or different. But that's just a book. Dad tells us to use both eyes when we meet people. First, use one eye to see if they understand the water. Second, use the other eye to see if they understand the land. Albert didn't seem to understand the land at all. Dad says that when people don't understand the land or the water, we need to be careful.

Mémèr taught me that things aren't always what they seem. That's an important teaching too. "Trust the feeling in your belly," she says. My belly tells me that Captain Rickley is a friend. And I bet he understands both the land and the water. I've never been afraid of snakes or captains.

Once Albert's close to the spur lines, he runs through the clearing, into the shack. I don't know for sure, but I swear he's peeking out through one of the holes in the wooden door. I bet I could ask him where Captain Rickley lives, but I don't want him to tell Florence and Ernest. He's just the kind of guy who would go running to tell them my secret plans.

I continue along the path to the swing bridge.

A skinny boy with short pants runs toward me.

"Hey!" I shout.

He stops. "What?"

"Do you know where I can find Captain Rickley?"

"Don't know him." He keeps running.

For the next while, I wait patiently as men cross back and forth on the swing bridge from the coal docks to Byng Inlet North. I ask each of them if they know the captain.

Finally, one man with a beard, covered head to toe in coal dust, says, "I've heard Captain Rickley has a camp along the Magnetawan River in the middle of town, about a ten-minute walk." He points.

Just then I see my brother William carrying some buckets from the coal docks toward the spur line yard. I dive into the long grasses near the water's edge.

When it's all clear, I run like a deer across the bridge and hide between two of the dormitories before William can spot me. If I move quickly enough, I'll have time to see Captain Rickley, ask my questions, and get back to town before Florence and Ernest notice I'm missing.

A loud boom echoes in the distance making the ground shake. What is that? It sounds like blasting. Maybe it's the war!

"Please, Pépèr. Please help me find Captain Rickley," I wish.

# 17

Captain Rickley's taller than a moose. He stands on the dock next to a small rowboat. How does that giant man fit in that small rowboat?

"*Bonjou*, Captain Rickley." I decide to use our home French instead of English or fancy French.

He turns around to see me standing on the land by the edge of the dock.

"Yer one of those kids that ran," he says in French. He speaks our French. Not the fancy French. He tilts his head and narrows his good eye at me. His glass eye catches the sun. Just in case the stories were true, I focus on his good eye.

"Sorry about that. Albert told us to run, so we did," I explain. "I don't know why."

"Used to town kids running by now. Just wanted to tell you all to be careful down by the shore of the Mag, eh. They're doing blasting with dynamite to recover the body of that young boy who drowned this morning. He got jammed in with the logs in a tight spot in the river."

"I heard about him. I didn't know kids could get jammed like that. How awful. It's all so very sad. Did you hear the loud blasts? I wondered if the war started."

Captain Rickley nods. He doesn't say anything at first. He looks at me for a long time. It makes me feel uncomfortable, so I look around.

"You're a girl," he says.

"Yes," I reply. I notice his small home looks like an ice fishing hut. A crooked sign on the door says Rickley. Keep Out. I wonder if I have made a mistake by coming here.

Then he starts to speak. "You're a brave girl. War? No chance. That's not started yet, although there's talk, but it's nowhere near Byng Inlet. Across the ocean. It would take more than a month by ship. Now, those sawmill tramways at Byng Inlet South aren't safe. Stay away from them. They just keep building them," he explains. "Nine of them there now. All these high tracks moving wood through the air from the mills to the train yard."

"What are they for?" I ask.

Along the shore, Captain Rickley has old ropes, buckets, stacks of bricks, cans, half pieces of furniture, piles of nets, and a big metal tub sitting on the rock with plants growing inside.

"Filling the pockets of rich guys from Toronto," he says. "Now get where you need to go. I've got work to do." Captain Rickley sits on a crate at the edge of the dock. He picks up a large net and works on untangling it.

I step onto the dock and take small tiptoe steps toward him until I'm directly behind him. I hold my breath and wonder what

I should ask next. Before I can speak, his arm reaches around, grabs me, and pulls me in front of him at the edge of the dock as he stands. My feet half dangle over the water.

"I thought I asked you to leave," he says.

"Okay, I'm sorry," I cry. "Please don't kill me."

"Kill you?" he asks. The sound of his booming voice echoes across the river and back again, giving me chills.

He holds me as easily as I hold a frog. And then it happens. I look right into his glass eye.

# 18

"So, girlie, what do you see when you look into the glass?" Captain Rickley pulls me toward him. My face is inches from his glass eyeball. "Not too many dare to look."

His eye isn't as scary as I thought it would be. I can see an entire world in his eye. I see the river and the sky. If I tilt my head, I can see myself. His eye is like a mirror one way and like nothing another way.

"I'm Bea. Louis's daughter. From the lighthouse," I offer. His eye isn't friendly, but it isn't angry either.

"Why didn't you say so in the first place?" Captain Rickley gently lowers my feet back to the dock and awkwardly pats my head. "Your dad and I grew up on these waters together. He's a good man."

"Dad knows everyone."

"I thought you were one of those town kids coming to mess with me. They're always daring each other to get close to spooky old Captain Rickley," he explains. "Do you want a maple candy? I have one inside."

Captain Rickley leads me from the dock to a spot in the shade between a spruce tree and woodpile. He goes into the hut and returns with a small glass dish of maple candy. He limps like every step hurts.

"I pick up this candy every week over at Henvey. I've got a sweet tooth, and there's a *Kookum* who always makes sure I have candies to feed it. Ha ha." He chuckles as he passes me the dish.

It tastes buttery and smooth, a little like the candy Dad makes us on the island, but Captain Rickley's candy has a strong maple flavor. In summers, Dad makes us his candy. He boils water in a pot over the fire. He adds brown sugar. He waits until the sugar's stringy in the water. Then he pours the mixture outside in a cool puddle in the granite. Then he pulls and pulls and pulls at it. He breaks off a piece of candy for everyone. Dad's candy tastes like caramels at Cornish's Store. I love all candy.

"It's amazing. Thank you."

"What are you really doing here?" Captain Rickley sets the candy dish on a stack of chopped wood. His voice is so deep it vibrates in my elbows.

"I need help, but it's a secret," I reply. "Have you seen gold out on the bay?"

"Sure, I've seen it. And nickel, mica, silver, copper, and quartz." He walks slowly to the dock. He continues to untangle a net.

"What does it look like?" I ask. "How will I know if I've seen it?"

"It's not what you might think. The gold is in the rocks. Here, come look at this." He drops the net and goes to a patch of rock by the hut. "Get down real close for a look."

I sit on the warm rock and focus my eyes as hard as I can to see gold.

He chuckles softly. "You won't see it there. Come, take a gander over here." He points to the rock beneath his feet. "The brown will be iron. The white is some sort of calcite, but this white is quartz. Now look real close for a bluish stain, do you see one? In the veins?"

"Is that one?" I crawl on my hands and knees over the rock for a closer inspection.

"That might be copper. Now move over to this one and see." He points to a bunch of rocks on the granite by the shore.

I pick up a rock the size of a baseball. I hold it up to the light as a line in it catches my eye. "This looks like gold!" I cry.

"Now look at it in the shade."

I move my hand to make shade and take the shade away, watching it turn from gold to brown to gold. "Oh, it's brown."

"Pyrite, not gold. You see, that's what you must watch for—gold will sparkle even in the shade." Captain Rickley goes behind the wood pile and picks up another small rock, testing it in the shade of his hand. "Try this one."

"It sparkles!" Finding gold this way isn't going to be easy. "So, I have to check every rock?" I ask. There are a lot of rocks on Georgian Bay.

"It's in the veins of rocks. Gold don't appear in those shiny bricks or coins like in the stories. Finding gold and mining gold require work. You can keep that," he says. "It might be gold, it might not."

I can't believe I might have real gold in my pocket.

"Thank you, Captain Rickley." I shake his hand properly like a grown-up. "You're not scary at all. This has been so helpful."

"Shh, don't tell the others." He smiles. "Now you better get where you need to before someone's worried about you."

# 19

I catch up with Florence and Ernest in Cornish's Store.

"Where've you been?" Ernest asks.

"Where's Eddie?" I ask.

"Gone fishing. He won't be back until tomorrow. His mom said he went out toward the bay early this morning. How did we miss him on the river?" Ernest's feet make flopping noises in the big winter boots as we walk around the shop.

"Because we left late?" I ask.

"Yeah, that's probably right." Ernest agrees.

"Mom wants flour, sugar, baking powder, lard, and some extra candles." Florence reads from a list.

"And our milk!" Ernest says.

"Yes, right. Milk," Florence says.

Mom always puts ten cents each in the purse for us to get our own pint of milk when we're in town. Dad says one day he'll buy a goat so we can have fresh milk whenever we want. It's so much tastier than dried milk. When I find the gold, maybe I'll buy a goat and a cow. Can you imagine having a quart of milk whenever you wanted?

I tap the rock Captain Rickley gave me. Maybe there's enough gold in this rock to buy a cow. I'm so excited I could scream.

We never buy milk with our money. Mom doesn't know we buy sodas instead. Florence and I get ginger ale, and Ernest gets root beer. William and Alcide prefer Coca-Cola.

We find a spot by the Magnetawan River to drink our sodas before heading to the Point. It's a bustle of activity on the river and on the land. Boats arrive and boats leave, everything from small rowboats like ours to big schooners. A couple of horses and buggies clip-clop from lower village to upper village. People walk on foot, pause to say hello even if it's someone they don't know. Some of the ladies wear fancy dresses with puffy sleeves. Some of the men wear ties and smart jackets. "Never trust a man in an ascot," Mom tells me and Florence all the time. "Hankies are for your nose, not your neck."

Kids run around singing songs in English I've never heard. Some kids fish with a line and pole from the riverbank. I watch quietly, taking it all in with fascination.

In winter, it's much quieter here. The coal docks and mills pause when the bay freezes. Many workers and their families leave town for the winter. Our family does the opposite. We come to town. We bring our huskies, Whiskey and Wine. We use a dogsled to pick up groceries or the mail. Little huts line the river for ice fishing. Sometimes we wear snowshoes to walk to school. And then, when everything melts, the river and the bay open again. Boats and workers stream into town. We move back out to the island, back to the lighthouse.

We walk slowly to the house on the Point. I learned so much from Captain Rickley about gold. Wait! Oh no! I was so excited about the gold, I forgot to ask him about the map. What good is knowing what gold looks like if I don't know where to find it? There are so many islands! Where will I find someone who can read the map now?

"Let's sneak over to the coal docks," Ernest suggests.

Florence puts the crate of groceries on the kitchen table. She passes William and Alcide their drinks. My brothers sit on wooden chairs in the living room, so they don't get coal dust on the other chairs with cushions. They're covered in coal dust, black from head to toe.

"I'm too tired to even sip, but I'll do it because it's so cold and delicious." Alcide takes the bottle of soda and despite being tired, gulps it down in three sips.

"I've had enough coal for today," William says.

"I'll go!" I offer.

"Come home before dark," Florence says. "And then a swim to wash off the coal."

"I'll swim in the morning," William says.

"Just let them have some fun, Flo," Alcide says.

Ernest and I waste no time in running out the door, across the swing bridge, and over to the big mounds of coal. We leave our shoes at home. We're lucky the house on the Point is so close. Our trick is that we swim home across the Still River. That way we clean the coal off and get home quickly.

The piles of coal look like mountains to me. They're huge. Alcide shares the story of coal every time we see a coal ship pass the lighthouse. A couple of years after the train tracks were opened, big coal ships started coming from Pennsylvania. The coal is dropped off by ships and then loaded onto steam locomotives to go all over Canada. On one side of the river in Byng Inlet South are most of the sawmills, and on the other side in Byng Inlet North are the massive coal docks. And none of this was here when Mémèr and Pépèr moved from Penetanguishene. I bet it was a lot of trees and quiet then.

"Race ya," Ernest challenges.

"You're on!" I reply.

We run up the hill of coal, slipping and scurrying to get to the top first.

"Yes!" I shout when I win.

"I'll beat you next time," Ernest says. "Ready? One, two, three."

We jump together and slide down the coal hill. It's not as fine as sand, nor as hard as stone.

A few other kids from town join us. No one really says much. We smile, race, and slide until it's nearly dark. Then we swim to the house on the Point.

# Part Four

## *The Cousins around the Fire*

# 20

The next day as William rows us home, all I think about is gold. Thankfully I remembered to take the map out of my pocket before we went to the coal docks to swim. I slipped it into my shoes at the house. If the map gets wet, the water will wash off the markings and I won't be able to read it to find the treasure. Now the map is safely tucked into my pocket again. I wonder which island the map leads to and what the different markings mean.

This is becoming more than an adventure. At first, I just wanted to be like the voyageurs, traveling in my *pti bato*, small boat, paddling from place to place, finding and sharing treasure. Now I think gold could really, really help my family.

I've come up with lots of reasons for why I need gold: to buy a house and land for Mom and Dad, to help my brothers so they don't have to work in dangerous places, to help my sister and I go to school to become teachers, and to buy a cow. Oh, and to buy some fabric for a new dress. A blue dress. And train tickets so Mémèr and I can travel to Waubaushene, where she was born, and she can tell me all about her life there. This list just keeps getting longer and longer. I'm going to need to find a lot of gold.

I take the rock from Captain Rickley out of my pocket and look at it.

"*Stunn bèl rawch*. Nice rock," Alcide says.

"Thanks." I smile. If only he knew.

The water is flat like a mirror. We travel quickly. When the river opens into the bay, the cooler air feels good. It's always so warm in town.

We hear laughter and then see trails of smoke rising into the evening sky from our island. This means we have company! I bet one of the cousins will be able to read my map!

"The big *bato*!" Florence shouts. "Dad said they were passing through soon."

"What a beautiful boat," Alcide says.

"*Bonjou!* Hello!" Ernest stands up on the bench and points. "I see it!"

The big old *cano dzu Nawr*, North canoe, is tied to a tree on the shore and floats out from the island. *Stun vyeu kano dékawrs dboulo*. It's an old birchbark canoe. They used this kind in the fur trade. I think every boat should have its own name. I'd name her *Bernice the Big Bato*, after me. We could paint *BBB* on the side. Dad says that boats are named after girls or wildlife. The cousins' boat is named *Seabird* and has a gull painted on either side of the bow. *Seabird* holds six rowers and has a small sail. Sometimes on their journeys, the voyageurs use the sail as a tent! I'd love to sleep in a North canoe.

"We're nearly there." William dips the oars into the bay, pushing and pulling with great force. The boat slices through the water even faster.

"There will be music tonight!" Ernest cheers.

We focus on the shore, trying to catch glimpses of our cousins.

William pulls up to the dock in the boathouse, and we can't climb out of the boat fast enough. Even the huskies come out to greet us, barking and running in circles as we rush to join the festivities.

Mémèr sits by the fire in her rocking chair. Whenever someone carries out Mémèr's rocker to the fire, it's a good party.

"*Bonjou*," Tony yells, running to hug each of us, starting with me. "You've gotten so old." He squishes me tightly in a bear hug.

The other cousins, a little younger than Dad, Ètienne, Robert, Amable, Jean, and Joe, run over too. They take turns lifting me up into the air and passing me from one to the next until I'm dizzy. They never bring their kids or wives on visits because they are usually paddling somewhere to work.

"Today is about the good stuff in life," Jean says to Florence. Florence *dans unn psit jig*, dances a little jig. Jean joins her.

"Boys, let's swim before we eat!" Amable cries out to my brothers.

They waste no time diving into the water. The cousins join them. I tuck the map into the toe of my shoe again. Soon Florence and I are swimming too—we all jump in wearing our clothes. Even Dad. Mom stands on the shore laughing with Mémèr.

## 21

The cousins always arrive with lots of fish. On the island, we mostly catch fish using a sturdy stick, a string of cotton, and a small hook. Our favorite fish to catch are whitefish and pickerel. I like to eat rock bass, but I don't like to catch them. The scales are so prickly and hurt my hands.

The cousins use big nets to catch fish, so they get more fish and bring a feast. With nets, they catch everything: rainbow trout, catfish, pike, perch, walleye. Then they throw back into the water any fish they don't want so the fish can continue living their fish lives. It's important to respect fish and only take what we need.

Tony and Amable clean the fish on the north side of the island. The guts go into the bay but in a different spot from where we swim. Dozens of gulls fly over our heads in circles, hoping to get a snack. We share with them. No part of the fish is wasted.

William and Ernest take turns running the cleaned fish over to Alcide, who dips the fillets into *unn shèyér*, a bucket with batter made from flour and beer.

Dad places the battered fillets in the sizzling lard in the frying pan over the firepit. The grill and the frying pan are balanced on stacked rocks set on either side of the flames.

When the fish is cooked, Dad heaps it in a pot with a lid. The pot sits on some hot rocks at the edges of the pit to keep warm. *Maman apawrt un pawt de binn.* Mom carries out a pot of baked beans. I'm in charge of plates and spoons. Florence fills the buckets for washing after we eat. It will likely be dark by the time we wash the dishes. The other cousins work on setting up camp for the night. Everyone has a job. Mémèr sits by the fire and softly plays the accordion while we work together.

Then around sunset, we sit on the rock to eat a feast of fish and beans.

"I love a big shore supper," Ètienne says.

"Wouldn't it be great to bring everyone together? The kids, our wives," Jean says. "Three, maybe four generations of our families together from all over the bay."

"Like this?" I ask.

"But much larger," Dad says.

"A hundred cousins," Tony says.

"And music," Amable says. "More fish?" He passes around the pot with the cooked fish.

"More beans, please!" Joe reaches across for the pot of beans. "You make the best beans in all of Georgian Bay, Cecilia."

"I've never had beans as good as these." Jean pats his belly and smiles.

"Imagine cousins from Penetanguishene, Sault Ste. Marie, North Bay, Manitoulin, maybe even Red River, all traveling to come together," Dad says.

"When can we have a big shore party?" I ask. It sounds wonderful.

Sunset passes, and the final moments of dusk hang onto every word around the fire.

"Sadly, it just isn't safe," Tony says.

"Why not?" William licks the bean sauce from his plate.

Tony closes his eyes to speak. "Our families have become like ghosts. Louis Riel fought for the rights of our people, and he was killed for it. The government called his work treason. They said he was a traitor and anyone who supported him was a traitor. How old were you when he died, Louis?"

I realize for the first time that Dad's first name is the same as Louis Riel's.

"*Livèr kton pér é tarivé en rakèt pour nou dawné lé nouvèl javè a peprè dzis zan.* I was about ten years old the winter your dad arrived by snowshoe to share the news," Dad says. "He traveled all that way so we would know."

"We were so worried," Mémèr whispers.

"After that, Sir John A. Macdonald, the prime minister, announced that people like us had to blend in with the settlers," Dad says.

Mémèr adds, "I think of the screech owl and how it blends into a tree as it watches in the woods. We weren't born with those gifts. It isn't easy to hide in plain sight."

"It's more like they try to erase us. The waters have changed since our dads worked the fur trade routes." Tony moves his arms as he talks. His voice grows louder. "Every year new rules, new laws. We are not fully French, nor are we fully Ojibway. We don't fit in either culture. When our parents lived together in

Drummond Island or our grandparents in Mackinac, none of that mattered. We belonged everywhere."

Jean adds another log to the fire. It sparks. "Many people choose to ignore the ways of our ancestor's because they don't understand us. Sometimes when people don't understand they get scared."

"And they introduce laws to protect what *they* know," Dad explains.

"They even changed your name!" Tony says.

"*Pour kwaw fér?* What for?" I ask.

"Just on paper. To keep his job, Pépèr changed the name Normandin to Lamondin," Dad says.

"Both names sound French to me," I reply. "So wait, is that why I'm Bernice Lamondin at school and you say Normandin when we're at home?" I just thought they were confused. Now I'm confused.

"Yes, Bea. That's right. And they are French names. For over a hundred and fifty years, Normandin has been a known voyageur name. Louis Riel's death changed things for us. To be lighthouse keeper, your Pépèr had to change his name, my name, or they would know our ancestry," Dad explains.

"If being French keeps my family alive, we will be French," Mom says.

"Are we safe?" Ernest asks.

"You kids have nothing to worry about on our island," Mom says.

"But it's good to be careful in town or at school," Dad says. "I'm sure people know who we are, yet they still expect us to pretend anyway."

Mom adds, "Just tell people you're French if they ask."

"But we are French," William says.

"And we are also Indigenous." Dad smiles.

"The laws demand us to forget that part, but you must always remember," Joe says.

"One day we may even lose our language," Tony adds. "They want us to speak that fancy French or English."

"It's not right. We are proud of our heritage, of who we are," Dad says.

"Survival of our families is the most important thing, so for now we live peacefully, like caterpillars. We do the best we can with what we have. We hold onto the hope that one day we will be butterflies," Mémèr says.

"*Marsi*, thank you." Tony walks over and gives Mémèr a hug.

"Let's sing our sadness." Jean picks up the fiddle and plays. The cousins nod and make sounds of agreement.

Robert sings a sad ballad about a ship lost at sea. His voice echoes along the rock, around the trees, and out into the bay. Florence adds a lovely harmony to the chorus. My eyes fill with tears. If anyone asks, I'll tell them it's the smoke from the fire. How can a song make me feel so sad?

I stare into the flames. Even though I don't fully understand, something important is being remembered tonight.

# 22

By the time the song ends, the fire has burned low. Darkness covers the bay. Our island feels very small. We are in a circle of faded light by the fire, a warm glow on the faces of my family. The night sky wraps us in a hug, holding us close to one another.

Mémèr sleeps in her rocker. Each time the fire pops, she wakes up. "Who's here? What did I miss?" she asks.

Everyone laughs.

"Looks like you have a crowd tonight, Auntie," Tony replies to Mémèr. He picks up the accordion. Jean and Joe reach for their fiddles. Alcide plays his fiddle too. Ernest and William play spoons they took out of the wash buckets.

This time the cousins share a lively song, filled with the happiness of living on the water. Florence and I sing and jig. Dad claps his hands and stomps his feet in time to the music. Mémèr taps her toe and rocks. We sing and dance for hours. Breezes wrap around us like a merry sash to unite the land, the water, and our family.

Once we've used up all our notes and our steps, we sit quietly under the stars. Mémèr reaches down for my hand. She speaks softly to the family. Since she is an Elder, everyone leans in and listens closely. "We know we are part of this land. We are proud of our ancestors. We have spirit like the water, shining. No one can take that away. Always remember who you are. Always shine."

"*Marsi*, Maamaa," Dad says. "Your words fill us tonight more than this feast of fish and beans."

"And now time for bed," Mémèr says. "Let's go, *ma pchi*." Mémèr taps me on the head, then runs her fingers through my hair. "Time to visit the mousey."

When I come back outside after helping Mémèr, Florence, William, and Mom have gone inside. Some of the cousins have gone to bed too. Alcide and Ernest linger by the fire softly playing fiddles together. Dad holds Mémèr's rocking chair under one arm as he stands on the path to the house with Tony and Jean.

They don't see me in the dark. I start to move sneakily to scare them, but then I realize they're having an important conversation. I take a step back to stay hidden and listen.

"You think there'll be work in the Soo?" Dad says. "The Soo" is another name for Sault Ste. Marie. Dad explained that to me once.

"Probably," Tony replies. "Robert heard Algoma Steel has some contracts."

"They've closed the mills at French River Village. Everything is being busted up. They've hired us every summer on contract for years, and now that's gone," Jean says.

"The mills will close in Byng Inlet too, just you wait. Times are changing, but we still have families to feed," Tony explains.

"Commercial fishing is out of control. We, who fish on a smaller scale, have less each year. Isn't life supposed to get easier?" Jean sounds angry.

"The way is always clearer in the morning, cousin," Dad says softly. "Let's get some rest."

Dad waves to my brothers to take the rocking chair inside, placing it on the rock for them. He walks with Tony and Jean to their tents. Then Dad pokes at the fire to be sure it burns out safely before going inside the lighthouse. I sneak into the house and up the ladder to our room and my bed.

Now I have something else to add to the list for when I find the gold: help my cousins. I can make sure that their families don't go hungry, and the dads don't have to move far away for work. We are lucky at the lighthouse. We always have everything we need. Dad doesn't need to leave home to get work. He is always here. There are plenty of fish to eat, and my family has shore picnics together all the time. We live freely on the island with only the laws of nature to guide us. Things like *don't go out when there's lightning* or *always check the winds before taking out the rowboat.*

We need to turn the sad stories into happy ones. This treasure hunt is a mission to help my family and my cousins.

# 23

Early in the morning, I see Tony at the firepit boiling water. Tony's gray cotton pants are rolled to just above his ankle. He's still in his white undershirt, his beige collared shirt draped across the woodpile. His hair is longer than Dad's, and this morning he has it tied back with a short sash. Tony sits on one of the long logs, rubbing his eyes.

I run to join him, but the rock is slippery from the morning dew. It's like ice. I slip and slide, wiping out within two steps of leaving the house.

"Easy does it," he says. "Good thing you kids are so bouncy. It's like you're made of rubber."

"Mom can boil water on the stove, you know." I play it cool and pretend I didn't just fall. I plunk down beside him on the log.

"Bea, why is the bay always on time?" he asks.

"Not another one," I groan. Tony's like a brother to Dad since his father was Mémèr's brother. He loves corny jokes and talks to me in puns. Secretly, I love it, but I don't want him to know.

"She likes to stay *current.*" Tony pours the hot water into his metal mug to make tea. "I heard you got that fancy cookstove. You're living the high life now. So happy it *panned* out."

"Dad says cooking eggs on it is hard," I reply.

"Oh yeah?" he asks.

"But I want them *over-easy.*" I try not to laugh.

"You got me, Bea. I walked right into that." Tony sips his tea. "We are not kindred spirits but *kindling* spirits."

I groan and smile. The warmth of the fire takes the dampness out of the air.

"*Marsi* for taking such good care of Mémèr," Tony says. He pokes at the fire with a stick. "She's lucky to have you here to watch out for her."

"She sleeps a lot," I share.

"She's grieving. He was the great love of her life. She must feel Pépèr here. His spirit is all around us. This is his island. He built this life for all of you. They both did," Tony explains.

I hug him.

"Tony, do you know anything about maps?" I ask.

"My dad taught me a lot about them," Tony says. "At one point he worked with surveyors, the ones who make the maps, to help them navigate the waters and islands."

"This is a secret map." I pull the map from my dress pocket. It's tearing in a few spots from being folded and unfolded so many times. Sitting next to Tony on the log by the fire, I pause. Is this a good idea? He's Dad's closest cousin. What if he tells Dad what I'm up to? Would Dad stop me from searching for the gold?

"A secret map. I specialize in that kind. Don't worry, we're nowhere near the cornfield," he says.

"Why should that matter?" I ask.

"Too many *ears*." He sips the last of his tea and sets the mug down on the rock. When I don't laugh, he says, "I can tell this is a serious map. Let's see. Let me help."

I unfold the map and pass it to Tony. As he looks at the map, I look around the area to be sure no one else is coming this way.

Tony holds the map up to the sun. He turns it around and flips it over. He carefully inspects it from every angle. "Okay," he says.

"Okay?" I ask. "What do you mean, 'okay?'"

"Where did you get this map, Bea? It's definitely a map." His smile fades, and he speaks in a low, soft voice. "A few things. First, those letters are in cursive. You will need someone who can read cursive to help you with figuring out these words. I think the place on the map is just south of here. You know the channel after Whitefish Channel. What's that one called?"

"Burritts Bay?" I ask.

"That's the one. Looks like there's an island there in the middle of the channel. Go past that nearly to the end of the bay and look for this tree on the south side. Do you recognize this tree?" Tony pulls the paper up closer to his face. "It looks familiar, but I can't remember its name."

"Slippery elm?" I ask. Mom's always telling me the names of everything whenever we go anywhere.

"Yes! I'm sure that's right. It's on the same island as three white pines," he says. "How far of a row is that from here?"

"Maybe half a day," I guess. "I'm not sure."

"Where did the map come from?" Tony asks. He passes it back to me then prepares another cup of tea.

"A man was here a few days ago. An artist named Tom Thomson. He left it behind," I explain.

"I don't know much about artists," Tony says. "Did he do the painting in the boathouse?"

"What painting?!" I jump up, stuff the map in my pocket, and run toward the boathouse. "Where in the boathouse?" I shout.

# 24

I run to the boathouse, so excited I nearly stop breathing. I scan the walls from floor to ceiling looking for a painting. Then I see it. There, leaning on the back of Dad's workbench, is a painting on a flat piece of wood. Has it been there all week? How did I miss it?

Approaching the painting like it's a great blue heron, I move slowly and carefully. This moment doesn't even feel real.

An island with a slippery elm and three white pines. The water and sky dance with colors.

I pull the map out of my pocket and hold it up to the painting. This is the spot! Not only do I have a map, but now I have a painting of this special place. My very own treasure island.

When I move my finger over the bumps and swirls of paint, it feels sticky. This painting is still drying. Did Tom give it to Dad? Or did he forget it here?

I sit on the dock, leaning on my elbows to stare at his painting: the trees, rocks, and water.

It's sort of like this painting is my family. The slippery elm can be Florence and the three white pines my brothers. The rolling granite and boulders are Mémèr and my parents. The water and sky around us, like the ancestors. And then I notice a fifth smaller tree in the painting. A young birch tree tucked in behind the slippery elm like it's spying on the others, just like me. This painting has a whole story inside of it. How did Tom capture my whole family in an island? He didn't even know us yet.

How will I sneak away to Burritts Bay without my brothers noticing? Florence is so busy she won't notice anything, but my brothers always keep track of the boats. They notice right away if a boat is missing. But now I know where to find the gold! And I have a map and a painting!

This is better than I could have hoped! The rest is just small details to figure out.

After breakfast, Tony joins me by the firepit again. He's dressed for traveling in his collared shirt and a blue vest. The cousins travel in style. Only his feet are still bare.

Tony says, "I never paddle long distances in boots."

I clean my teeth by putting some cooled wood ash on my finger and rubbing it on my teeth. He cleans his too. The other cousins finish packing up camp and load the canoe with their gear.

Tony sips water and spits the wood ash into the bush nearby. "Thank you for honoring me with your secret map, Bea. Did you find the painting?"

My speech is mixed up because my finger is still in my mouth. "The painting was just like the map, only better!" I exclaim. I sip water and spit in the same bush.

"Who can read that cursive for you?" he asks.

"Florence is the only one that can read cursive. But she never keeps secrets. She tells Mom and Dad everything," I explain. The last thing I want to do is involve Florence in this.

"If you can't trust your family, Bea, who can you trust? I bet she'd understand this is important." Tony removes the sash from his head and fluffs his hair with his fingers. "Do you have everything you need to go to Burritts Bay?"

"I can take the small rowboat." I realize I still haven't told him about the gold, about why I want to go to the island.

"Bring Alcide or William with you. It's much too far for you to go on your own, and there's open water to cross. Make sure you tell your mom and dad where you are going. Pack cups, a snack, matches, maybe a fishing pole. And you'll need this." Tony passes me his *sintsur fléché*, his sash.

"Your special sash?" I pass it back to him. "It was your dad's. It's yours."

"He wore this sash, or what's left of it, during his last paddle to deliver furs to Lac Seul. It's nearly fifty years old. Did you know that Auntie made it for him? Your mémèr. Every paddler needs a sash. It's the most useful tool of them all. Wrap it around the head and it's a hat. Tie it around the waist and it helps you portage because it gives your back support. Use a thread from the fringe to sew your dress. Tie up the boat when you can't pull it on shore. Even a pillow if you roll it up. Best of all, this sash will keep you safe. It's connected to your ancestors and your family." Tony ties the sash around my waist like Pépèr used to wear his.

"Girls don't wear them like that!" I exclaim. Girls wear the sash over one shoulder, across the body.

"Says who? This will give you strength too. You have an important life ahead." Tony stands back, admiring me in his old sash.

"Thank you! I always wanted a sash." The bright red and colorful arrowhead pattern fill me with joy. It's more beautiful than anything else I own. I love color so much.

"I want to leave a piece of my family story, our family story, here with you. You are the youngest cousin. One day, it will be up to you to share this with the next generation." He pats me on the head. "Take good care of this gift, Bea."

"*Marsi* for this special gift." I hug him as tightly as I can. Then he lifts me high above his head and carries me on his shoulders to the dock.

# Part Five

## *The Sewing Needle*

# 25

The last embers of the morning fire are the only reminder of the cousins' visit. Waves and gulls replace our songs and stories. Everyone's doing chores again.

I sit on the steps by the kitchen looking out at the water, thinking about the island with the gold. So far, I know what gold looks like, that the island is in Burritts Bay, and that the squiggles on the map are cursive writing. Once I talk to Florence about the cursive writing on the map, then I can row for the gold.

My fingers trace patterns on the sash. Each strand holds a different story. A cluster of monarchs fly around the wildflowers sprouting between the cracks in the rock. One of them lands on the sash and looks at me.

"What's it like out there, butterfly?" I ask. "Can you take me with you?"

"Who are you talking to, *ma pchi*?" Mémèr asks through the screen on the door.

"The butterflies," I reply.

"And what do they say?" she asks.

"That I should grow some wings and fly," I reply. "I wish I could go to the Soo."

"And what would you do there?" Mémèr opens the screen door.

"Sing and dance with the cousins."

"Well, we can do that here. Time for your lesson," she says.

"I can already sing and dance." I stand up and face her, my hands on my hips.

"Your beading lesson," she explains. "Let's go. No more moping." She takes the cloth from me and looks at the stitching as we make our way to the living room. "Is this Philip's old sash?"

"Tony gave it to me."

"Tony's maamaa is from Red River. After she married my brother, she moved to Waubaushene but missed her family. They went to visit every year. Such a long journey. Tony's a good man, like his dad: my brother." Mémèr returns the sash. I tie it around my waist.

"He said to wear it like this." I spin around to make the fringe float. Blue, yellow, red, green, white. All the colors blur as I move.

"What a special gift. We give the sash to those we care about most. I haven't made one in many years. When I was your age, Auntie taught me how to finger weave. We didn't all go to school like you, but we learned good things from our kin like beading, sewing, finger weaving, cooking, all sorts of interesting things about plants and medicines. We were always learning. I still learn something new every day."

"Did anyone go to school?" I ask.

"Pull my rocker by the window, *ma pchi*, so I can see better in the light. My brother Charlie went to school, but it was far away near Rice Lake with the Michi Saagiig Anishinaabeg. He could read and write so well too. We all could, but he could read so fast."

I drag the rocker over and put the basket by her feet. Mémèr's basket smells good even though it's old.

"I made that out of sweetgrass," she explains. "An old woman on Christian Island helped me." Mémèr opens the basket. It's a mess of scraps of fabric, hide, and needles stuck in small cushions. She pulls out a cedar box filled with glass beads. She passes me a spool of thread and a pair of scissors. "Pull the thread so you have double the length from your fingertips to your shoulder."

"*Kawm saw?* Like this?" I pull the thread from the spool across my body. The spool's slippery and falls, rolling halfway across the room.

"Oh, *ma pchi*, roll it back up," Mémèr says. She closes her eyes and leans back in the rocker. "Wake me when you're ready."

I wind the thread around the spool again and then stretch the thread across my body until it's the right length. "Done."

Mémèr opens her eyes and passes me the scissors. "Okay, now cut."

I cut the thread and put the scissors down.

Mémèr passes me one of the needles. "Next, thread this needle. Put the thread through the eye, that hole right there. Then you can thread another needle for me. We each need one." She puts the other needle into the side of her mouth.

"Mémèr, why did you put a needle in your mouth?" I ask.

She removes the needle to talk. "An old sewing trick. You'll thread this one next." She rests it in the side of her mouth again. Mémèr uses her hands to sort through the basket, selecting what we need.

I focus on threading the needle. It isn't as easy as it looks to get the thread through the eye. *Okay, Bea, let's not prick fingers this time,* I tell myself.

"Got it!" I jump in celebration.

Mémèr says, "Good, *ma—*" She brings her hands up to her neck. Her eyes are huge. The needle! Mémèr swallowed the sewing needle!

# 26

"Help!" I shout. "Mom! Dad! Anyone?! Help!" I run in circles. What do I do? Mémèr's frozen, her eyes growing larger and larger. "You need to breathe, Mémèr."

Why is no one coming? Is Mom outside washing the clothes? I run to the window and yell. "Maamaa! *A lèd!* Help!" Where's Dad? Maybe he's up the tower. I saw him carrying a jug of oil earlier. I climb to the landing on the second level of the tower and shout up to the top. "Dad! Come quickly! It's Mémèr!"

As I climb back down the ladder, my foot slips, and I hit my mouth on one of the steps.

Florence arrives first. "What happened?" she asks. "You're bleeding." She runs toward me.

"Mémèr swallowed a sewing needle," I cry.

She looks at Mémèr. "Oh my! I'll get Mom." Florence runs outside.

Dad scrambles down the ladder to the living room. "Bea! What happened?"

"It's Mémèr...threading a needle...her mouth and...." I breathe so fast it's hard to talk.

Dad looks at Mémèr. Her huge eyes tear up.

"Open your mouth, Maamaa," Dad says. He looks inside. "I can't see it. You must have swallowed it."

Mom and Florence come running into the house. My brothers are close behind them.

Dad puts his hand on Mémèr's forehead for a moment. Her body relaxes. She looks more comfortable. Then Dad puts a hand near her throat. Mémèr closes her eyes.

"We'll have to take her to town. Alcide, get the boat ready." Dad picks up Mémèr in his arms like she's a small child.

William holds the door open. "Will she be okay?"

"We need to get her to a doctor. Maamaa, don't talk. Just rest. Cecilia, you come with me to watch her in the boat. Alcide and Florence, keep things under control here." We all follow as Dad moves swiftly to the boathouse and gently places Mémèr into the belly of the boat, sitting on the floor with her back against the bench.

Mom sits on the bench in the boat near Mémèr. She covers Mémèr with a blanket and caresses her head. "Don't worry, Mémèr. You'll be just fine. We'll get you to the doctor."

As they row toward town, I stand on the dock sobbing. Ernest stands beside me holding my hand.

"We need to clean up that blood," Florence says, wiping my face. "Show me your teeth. Are they all still there?"

I don't even know how we moved from the dock to the kitchen through to the living room.

Florence pushes me into a wooden chair. "Open your mouth, Bea. It's going to be okay. Dad will make sure of it." She looks inside my mouth. "How is it that you're bleeding? Mémèr was the one to swallow the needle."

"Tripped." I'm too devastated to speak.

She gives me a glass of water. "Drink this," she says. She finishes cleaning up my face. "Just sit here for a minute and catch your breath."

Mémèr's basket is out, and her rocker is by the window. Everything is just as we left it. All that's missing is Mémèr. I start crying again. Florence goes to work putting the room back in order, returning the rocker to its place and tidying up the basket.

William comes down the steps carrying the big empty kerosene jug. "Light should be good until tomorrow," he says. Then he continues out the door.

"I'm going to make you some tea. We'll have a scone with jam. That will help." Florence goes to the kitchen.

I decide to join her and sit at the table on one of the benches. We have a large kitchen table made from a big plank of pine. There is a bench along each side and a chair at each end. Ernest comes in and sits across from me on the other bench.

Florence continues to fuss. "You're in shock, Bea. That's all. It will pass. You'll be okay." Florence uses the hand pump at the sink to fill the kettle and sets it on the stove.

Our new cookstove is white, like our cupboards, with a black top and a special spot just for the *tékér*, the kettle. It has a big range up over the top too. Mom loves that part. Florence gathers some wood from the pile near the stove, loads the stove, and lights it, closing the little stove door once she sees flames. She pulls out two cups for tea and scoops some loose tea into the teapot. It's helpful to watch her move around the kitchen.

Florence finds some scones in the cupboard. She spreads butter and jam on the pieces before placing the plate in the center of the table.

Ernest grabs a piece of scone. "Thanks!"

"Hey, that's for Bea!" Florence says.

"She can't eat all that," he says.

"Yeah, you're right. I added some for us too. I think we're all in shock." Florence sits in Mom's chair at the end of the table and eats a piece too.

"Don't worry, Bea. The scone will soak up any blood left in your mouth." Ernest smiles.

The kettle whistles. Florence takes another cup out for Ernest. The three of us sit there in silence with our tea.

# 27

The next day just after dark, we wait on the rock, watching the water for hours and jumping every time we see or hear a boat. The hot, sticky air makes every minute feel like an hour. Usually there's a breeze in the evening, but even the bay holds its breath waiting to hear if Mémèr's okay.

I hear the oars dip into the water. Sound travels so fast across the bay. Soon I see the outline of a boat.

"Well, isn't this a nice welcome," Dad says as he pulls to shore. He's alone.

"Where's Mémèr? And Mom?" Alcide asks. He grabs the boat as it floats toward the dock and holds it in place as Dad climbs out. Florence holds a lantern. William helps Alcide tie the boat.

"She's okay but needs to go to Parry Sound. Your maamaa went with her." Dad puts his arms around me and Florence. We walk to the house together.

"Where's Parry Sound again?" I ask.

"About an hour south of here by train," Dad says.

"Why didn't she go to the Byng Inlet hospital island down the river?" William asks.

"We tried. They can't help her. The hospital is only for the mill workers and their families, and since I don't work for the lumber company anymore, Mémèr can't be treated there," Dad says.

"We can't use the hospital? That doesn't seem right," Alcide says.

"We saw the doc at his office in town. Your maamaa will take good care of your mémèr too. Parry Sound has a bigger hospital. It'll be okay." Dad goes into the kitchen. "What's for supper?"

"We have some fish in the icebox," William says.

"I'll just make some oatmeal. Anyone else?" Dad asks.

We sit around the kitchen table late into the night, no one speaking much, eating oatmeal with maple sugar.

# 28

Three dreadfully long days pass, and we hear nothing from Parry Sound. Alcide and William went to stay at the house on the Point in town. They could work at the coal docks each day and row across the river to check in at the Byng Inlet post office for a telegram. When they hear news, they are instructed to row out to Dad at the lighthouse right away.

The mood at the lighthouse is grim. Dad even tells one boatload of visitors we're closed for tours. He's never done that before. I'm too distraught to even think about my map or the painting or the gold. I sleep a lot. I wake up crying in the night, seeing Mémèr's eyes pop and her hands holding her throat in my dreams.

After lunch on the third day, Ernest and I sit up in the rafters of the boathouse playing cards. It's raining, and neither of us want to be in the house. It's empty without Mémèr and Mom.

Dad's out filling the kerosene at the range lights because my brothers are in town. Florence tries to keep up with all her chores and Mom's chores, but it isn't easy. I'm too sad to help her.

"Oy, up there!" Dad yells. He rows into the boathouse.

Ernest and I scramble down the beams.

"Any news?" Ernest asks as he grabs Dad's boat to pull it into the dock. We ask this question every time we see Dad.

"They've gone to Toronto," he says. He's white as a gull. "Your brothers will be home soon. They're going to catch some fish for dinner. I met them out on the water. Ernest, make sure you get that wood piled. I can see you haven't gotten to it yet."

"Toronto?!" I cry. "Why?"

"They have some sort of a machine there called an X-ray. Mémèr and your mom went on the train to Toronto General Hospital a couple days ago. The doc thinks the needle is in her appendix but wants to be sure before they operate, take her appendix out maybe. This X-ray machine will be able to look through her skin to see the needle. I don't even believe it." Dad climbs out of the boat.

"Operate? Take something out! She could die!" I panic.

"I know, Bea. It's not good." Dad stops by the messy woodpile. "We're going to need more wood too, Ernest."

"Why couldn't you fix Mémèr?" Ernest asks. "You know, use your healing?"

"My medicine isn't strong enough to remove a sewing needle," Dad says. "This is bigger than an ache or a pain."

"Do you think Mémèr will ever come back?" I whisper through my tears.

Dad picks me up in his arms. "Bernice, your mémèr has the strongest spirit of anyone I know. We need to have faith that everything will work out the way it needs to. She wouldn't want us worrying like this."

He kisses my head and puts me back down on the rock.

"When will she be back?" Ernest asks.

"I guess we wait and see," Dad says. "For now, the woodpile."

The gold means even more now. I need to help my family. If we had the gold, maybe we could all take the train to Toronto to be with Mémèr and Mom. We wouldn't have to be apart. I feel more certain than ever that I am meant to find this gold, and it's going to change everything for us.

# 29

One afternoon I go to the spot on our island where Mémèr talks to Pépèr. Sitting on the granite with Mémèr's rock against my back, I watch waves splash onto the shore. My hair scatters in all directions in the wind. We haven't heard anything from Toronto. Dad says no news is good news.

"Pépèr. Are you out there?" I shout into the bay. "We need help. Please bring Mémèr back to us." I pull some tobacco from my pocket, stand up, and walk to the edge. I throw tobacco to the water the way Mémèr does to offer thanks, using my left hand because it's closest to my heart. The wind catches it and blows it all back at me. Uh-oh. This isn't a good sign. "Sorry! Can you still help anyway?" I ask the bay. "Please and thank you. I love you."

Each evening before dark I visit the painting in the boathouse. I moved it to a spot up in the rafters so I can look at it more closely. Everyone's so busy with Mom and Mémèr gone that they haven't noticed the painting's moved. I stare at the painting for hours, imagining Mémèr is there hiding behind one of the trees. If I look at it long enough, she'll pop her head out, smile, and say, "Who's there? What did I miss?"

"We miss you, Mémèr," I say into the wind.

A crow lands on the rock by me and caws.

"Hello, Crow." I twist around.

Crow continues to caw and waddles closer to me. It tilts its head.

"Is that you?" I ask.

"*Caw,*" says Crow.

"Where have you been all this time, Crow?" I step closer.

*"Caw, caw."*

"You're so big! It's me. Bea."

Crow stretches out its wings and flies closer. "Bea-the-Bean," she says.

"Oh my! It is you!!" I exclaim. I haven't seen Crow in years. That's her name. Crow. When Crow was a baby, her wing was hurt. Dad helped me feed her small pieces of scone soaked in water. We cared for her until she healed and was strong enough to fly. She followed me everywhere for an entire summer until she flew away one day when I was at school.

When I was a baby, my brothers thought I looked like a bean. They started calling me Bea the Bean. They said it over and over for years. Even Crow learned my name. But it feels like a baby name, and I'm growing up. So now I tell my brothers they can call me Bernice or Bea, but not Bea the Bean. Crow can call me Bea the Bean. Crow has permission.

*"Caw, caw. Caw."* Crow goes to the rock again.

"Have you been to Toronto?" I ask. It's worth a try. She has wings after all.

*"Caw."*

"Does 'caw' mean yes or no?"

"Bea-the-Bean."

I laugh. "That isn't any clearer." Reaching into my dress pocket, I pull out a small piece of bannock. I hold it for Crow. She nibbles at the pieces on my hand.

"I'm worried about Mémèr. If any of your friends are in Toronto, ask them to check on her," I plead.

As I head back to the lighthouse a while later, Crow follows me.

"Crow is back!" Ernest runs over to meet me as we walk up the path.

"I think she's hungry. She ate all the bannock I had in my pocket."

"I'll get more bannock." Ernest skips into the lighthouse.

I walk to the boathouse to pick up an old metal bowl we used for her water last time. Crow follows me, happily cawing all the way like she's having a conversation. I go to the bay and fill the bowl with water. Even though there are puddles and there is the whole big Georgian Bay, I think Crow likes having her own bowl of water.

Ernest returns with pieces of bannock in each hand. He is also chewing some. He lines up the bannock on the rock near the bowl of water. Crow dances around the feast before eating every piece.

"I've missed Crow," Ernest says. "Do you remember the time she pooped on Florence?" He flails his arms and runs in circles pretending to be Florence.

"That was so funny! Florence was mad!"

"I wonder if Crow still finds the best blueberries. Do you remember?" Ernest reveals more bannock from his pocket and breaks some pieces to put near the bowl of water.

"*Caw, caw,*" says Crow. She pecks at the snack.

"We followed her for an hour in the bush. We had so many mosquito bites and scratches because there was no real path. Then, bam. Blueberries everywhere. It was the most blueberries I've seen in my entire life," I exclaim.

"We ate so much!" Ernest says. "We should go back there."

"Then you tried to get her to deliver messages to Eddie in town, tying little scrolls to her foot. Dad caught you though! He was so mad," I tease.

"I didn't know Crow and Dad were friends too!" Ernest bellows. Just then Dad's boat approaches.

We burst into big belly laughs.

Crow stops her feast and flies to meet him on the water. Crow sits on the bow of the boat. I can hear that he's talking softly, but I can't make out the words. What secrets do they share?

"Crow's back!" Dad says when he pulls into the dock. "When did she get here?"

"She found me today!" I reply.

"Well, I have some good news! Mémèr is going to be okay. They removed her appendix in Toronto. The sewing needle is out! Once she's strong enough, they will take the train home." Dad jumps out of the boat. Ernest ties it for him.

Dad picks me up and swirls me around. "My women are coming home!" he cries. Then we dance a jig, right there on the rock without music.

# Part Six

## *The Blueberries and the Bears*

# 30

Florence and I pick blueberries on the south side of the island. Crow marches like a guard. I'm determined to talk to my sister today about the cursive writing in the map.

"Crow will keep those rattlers away," I declare. "Right, Crow?"

"*Caw*," Crow replies.

"Say Florence." I sing. "Florence. Florence."

"*Caw*," Crow replies.

"Bea!" Florence says.

"Bea-the-Bean," Crow says.

Florence laughs.

"I'm training Crow to say your name," I reply. "Flor-ence. Say Flor-ence."

*"Caw."*

Mom taught us to check for rattlers by tapping the bushes with a stick before we stick our hands in to pick the berries. I tap the bush.

"We'll practice making a pie today," Florence says. She squats by a blueberry bush and picks quickly, placing each one into the pot. Neither of us could find the berry baskets so we're using pots from the kitchen to collect the berries. "We can make a blueberry pie for when Mémèr and Mom come home."

"I love your pies!" I move to a squishy patch of thick moss beside a blueberry bush. One berry goes into the pot, one berry goes into my mouth. They're warm and juicy. The perfect balance of sweet and sour.

Florence catches me eating a berry. "Hey! We'll be here all day if you eat them now."

"That's why I came!" I laugh. It's easy to make my sister mad. "Flor-ence," I say in the voice of a crow.

"Dad thinks they might be home in a week. I wonder what it's like in Toronto," Florence muses.

"Do you think they have indoor toilets?" I ask.

"Muriel told me she went to Toronto once to visit a cousin and they have motor cars. No horse and buggies or dogsleds, but something on wheels that drives over the paths," she explains.

"Alcide was telling me about motor cars one day. People at the coal docks talk about them all the time. And something called electricity. It makes lights!"

"See, look at this cluster." Florence points to some blueberries. "Why can't I make them look like that in my embroidery? Wait, did you hear that?"

"What?" I imagine stretching my ears for a better listen.

"Shh." Florence freezes, her eyes widen.

"Where did Crow go?" I whisper.

"Shh." Florence slowly stands.

I stand too. Then I see something move in the trees.

"There," I point. We take a step toward the noise. We can't see what's among the trees.

"At your feet!" Florence shouts.

A large brown snake with a pattern on it. I hold my breath as my eyes follow its body to the tail. "It's a fox snake. Thank goodness. No rattles." I reach to pick it up from the middle of its body, holding it carefully with two hands. "Let me move this away from our blueberry bush."

"Something else. Did you hear that?" Florence asks. She takes a step toward the small section of woods. Then another step.

With the fox snake in my hands, I take a step too.

A twig snaps.

Florence charges into the woods. "Gotcha!" she yells. It all happens quickly, and then Florence returns to the clearing, dragging two brothers: Ernest and William. Crow flies behind them.

"Florence!" Ernest cries.

"Florence!" William shouts.

"Flor-ence. Flor-ence," Crow says.

We laugh. Finally, Crow speaks!

"Did you lose something?" I offer them the snake.

"You were supposed to think it was a rattler," Ernest says.

"I thought for sure you were going to scream." William gently takes the fox snake from me. "We'll put Foxy back where we found it."

Defeated, the boys return through the woods. Crow follows them saying "Flor-ence" over and over.

# 31

"Brothers," Florence says.

"They do the same thing every time. Snakes or worms. Fish. Anything slippery." I pick up my blueberry pot and eat a couple of berries.

"We screamed one time." Florence returns to picking berries. "Maybe it was two times we screamed. Or three."

"Ten." I hold up ten fingers. "But not today!"

"From surprise more than anything else. At least that's what I tell myself," Florence says.

"We should go around to the other side of the island and try another spot, *Flor-ence*." I pop another blueberry into my mouth.

"Hey! Right! Crow said my name!" Florence replies. "Amazing!"

We walk quietly over the granite paths, around juniper, sumac, and cedar bushes. Sometimes we jump over puddles formed in the dips in the rock. I continue to sneak a blueberry taster from the pot every once in a while.

"Hey, Flo?"

"Yes, Bea?"

"Can you read cursive writing?" I ask.

"Absolutely. I was the best cursive writer in my class," she says. "Why?"

"Just wondering, that's all." I lose my nerve.

"You'll learn next year," she says.

"For sure. Just wondering if you can—"

"Look! Our old moss playhouse!" Florence cheers, and she runs ahead.

Some of the moss is thick and soft, squishy like a mattress. Some of the moss is hard and curly, stuck to the rock like peeling scales or snakeskin. We love the squishy moss.

I run at the thick moss like it's a pile of leaves and then roll into it. My pot of blueberries spills, rolling across the granite.

"Blueberries!" Florence yells.

"Sorry!" I reach for rolling blueberries to add them back to my pot without crushing them. I was so close to telling Florence about the map. Does this mean I should wait? Do I try again? Will she keep my secret? Oh gosh. Who can she tell? Mom isn't even here. She's all the way in Toronto. Now, I'm making this all more difficult than it needs to be. Right? Tony says I need to trust my family.

"We haven't played here in a couple years." Florence walks around the area. "I can't believe our rooms are still as we left them. This was the kitchen." A wall of moss surrounds her, stacked half a foot high, like in a floor plan. There is an opening and a stick angled on the rock like the shadow of a door. "And this was Mémèr's bedroom," she says.

"You pretended to take naps," I laugh.

"While my little sister did all the work!" She wanders to a pile of rocks in our play kitchen.

"Why did we stop coming here?" I ask.

"I don't know. Doesn't look like anyone has been here since," Florence says.

We meander around the rooms, their borders sketched out with moss we peeled from the granite in other places.

"Our mansion on the island." I spread my arms proudly.

"Bigger than old Bigwood's," Florence adds.

"Looks like someone visited the parlor." I point at a huge pile of bear scat, fresh and blue.

"That bear's been eating our blueberries!" Florence scolds.

"Looks like it's from today." I look around but only see trees, rock, water, and the lighthouse far off on the other side of the island.

"Hopefully the bear swam over to another island by now."

"I need your help with something, but you can't tell anyone." Sitting on a small rock in the living room of the moss house, I twist a stick around on the granite like it's a pencil making patterns on the rock.

Florence stretches out on a patch of spongy moss watching the clouds. "Whatever you need, Bea. Sisters help each other," she says.

The sun burns high above us. I can feel its heat from the sky and from the rock. A slight breeze moves across the bay over the island, keeping us cool in the sun.

"Can you read some cursive for me?"

"Oh, that's easy. Show me when we get home," she says.

"I have it here, in my pocket," I reply. Slowly, I pull the folded map from my pocket. It's looking more worn now.

The paper's flimsy and permanently creased along the fold lines. Some fingerprints, water stains, and the guts of one spider soil its once perfect condition.

Florence doesn't move and waits for me to bring her the map. I sit next to her. It feels like a dramatic moment. I can almost hear Alcide's fiddle playing a scary tune in the back of my mind.

She looks at the map carefully and slowly, turning it this way and that way. Her face is expressionless on purpose, I'm sure. "What's this? Where did you get it?" she asks. Her voice is flat. She looks at me, her eyes squinting and serious, with only a hint of a twinkle. This is why I don't want to show Florence. She makes everything so annoying.

"Can you tell me what it says first? Then I'll tell you the story?" I ask.

"Nope. You first," she says. She holds the map high over our heads, dangling it in the breeze.

I think quickly. "You know, maybe if we both share our information, we can solve the mystery together."

"Hmm...well, you're going to need to pay then. Chores. My choice." She folds the map, puts it in her pocket. She uses her best negotiator's eye gaze.

"Fine. I choose the chores." I raise my eyebrows and lock eyes with her. I imagine my eyes have the ability to make her agree to whatever I say. It never works, but I always try.

"Nope. My choice. You will pluck the duck the next time Dad wants one for supper. And you will finish picking the blueberries today while I do nothing." She smiles. Florence hates plucking the feathers off ducks. I'm not a big fan either, but it sure is nice to eat duck sometimes instead of fish every day.

"Fine." We shake hands. "Tell me everything, then I'll tell you everything." I squish in closer to her.

Florence takes the map out of her pocket and studies it again. "I don't really understand what it means. But, here, these words say *burnt umber*. And there, *cadmium*." Florence explains. Her nose crinkles when she doesn't understand something.

"Burnt. I only know one word. Are you sure it says umber? Maybe it's burnt under?" I ask.

"I'm certain, Bea. I just don't know what it means. This over here says *cerulean*. Sounds like a lake creature. Oh, and this last one says *sienna*. Makes me think of snakes. The next snake we meet, we'll name it Sienna. Such a beautiful name. Sienna snake slithers through the sandy stone on the shore."

"Maybe it's a code? Or food. Or...oh gosh, this is hard!" I lie in the moss, staring up at the clouds.

Florence lies beside me. "Your turn, Bea. Anyway, what is this paper?"

"Tom left it behind. I think it's a map," I whisper.

Florence belly laughs, rolling on the moss. "What? Don't be ridiculous. How can this be a map? Have you ever even seen a map before?"

"There was a map in my book *Treasure Island*." I pout.

"Where does it lead? What is it a map to?" she asks.

I stare at the clouds sliding by and wonder what to say next. If I tell Florence the map is for gold, I may never hear the end of it. She'll want to tell our brothers, and then my secret disappears. The whole story changes. I decide to say as little as possible. "That's what I'm trying to figure out."

"Bea, you're fibbing! You know more than you're telling me." Florence moves quickly and pins me to the moss. She sits on my stomach, holding down my arms over my head. "If you don't tell me more, I'm going to tickle your armpits until you cry!" she threatens.

"Fine! It might be a map to Burritts Bay." I wiggle to break free, but she's too strong.

"And how do you know that?" she says.

"Mémèr found it when Tom left. It sort of matches the painting in the boathouse, and the painting shows an island that might be in Burritts Bay." I search my brain for details I can share that will make her think she knows everything.

"And…." Florence releases her grip on my arms. "One more detail, and you're free. Fair is fair. Why do you want to know what the words mean?"

"Maybe the words are clues?" I ask. "I'm trying to figure it out."

Florence rolls on the moss beside me. "Maybe something burned. Did anything burn over in Burritts Bay? I don't think so. Dad might know. Or Alcide fishes over there sometimes."

"It's a secret, Flo. Please promise not to tell anyone," I beg.

"Who could I possibly tell?" She flutters her eyelashes.

"I'll even share the treasure with you." I was trying so hard not to say the word *gold* that *treasure* just popped out.

"Treasure?! Bea! Do you think this is a treasure map? How exciting!" she squeals.

"It's a secret," I reply.

"It will be so helpful for Mom and Dad if you find treasure. Alcide said he heard talk in town. There will be a big bill when Mom and Mémèr come home. The train tickets, surgery, and the hospital. Mom even had to rent a room in Toronto while she was there. I bet Dad will have to ask Mr. Bigwood to lend him some money."

"If it is treasure, which I don't know for sure that it is, of course I'll help Mom and Dad. They don't have money for all that." I add more to the list of what I'll do with the gold when I find it.

# 32

"We need to figure out what those words mean. Maybe we could ask Dad?" Florence asks.

"Remember, it's a secret!" I repeat.

"Yes, yes, yes." She nods.

"It may just be a picture like you said." I try to recover from blurting out the real story.

Florence sings, "You think it's treasure. You think it's treasure." She dances around me.

I roll over onto my belly. My face is in the moss. This is the worst. She knows about my adventure for two minutes, and she's already ruining it.

"Bea," she whispers.

I ignore her.

"Bea," she whispers again.

I lie still.

"Bea." Florence kicks me in the leg.

"Ouch! Come on, Flo!" I roll over to see where she is so I can kick her back. I gasp. Standing in the clearing, up on two legs, is a huge black bear. It takes a step toward us, still on two legs.

"That's not what I expected!" I whisper-shout to Florence.

The bear takes two more steps toward us. Florence falls back into the moss. We wiggle to sit closely together, our knees to our chests, arms wrapped around our knees.

It growls. I feel it vibrate in my toes and back and nose. I stare at the bear. The bear stares at me. I hold my breath.

The bear tips down to its four feet and smells the rock near our feet. I think I feel its breath on my bare toes. I'm frozen. I can't move or think.

"Flor-ence. Flor-ence," says Crow. "Flor-ence."

The bear looks up at Crow, flying circles above us, low enough that Bear could swing a paw and hit Crow. Is Crow teasing the bear? Has Crow come to save us from being eaten?

*"Caw, caw, caw-caw, caw-caw."* Crow speaks a language we don't understand.

Bear looks at us, looks at Crow. Bear meanders on all fours over to Florence's pot of blueberries, licks inside the pot. In two bites she eats all the blueberries Florence spent hours picking. Then Bear follows Crow. They go south toward the shore. We don't speak or move.

Just as they are out of sight, three cubs emerge from the bush. They walk by as though we're not here, following Mama Bear and Crow. Four bears in one afternoon! Hopefully Crow will lead them to the shore so they can swim to another island. When they are gone and we can see Crow in the air, far off in the distance, we relax.

"Breathe, Bea," Florence says.

I let out a giant breath and fall back, exhausted.

"Crow saved us," I whisper. "Crow said your name."

Florence wipes tears from her eyes. "You and your silly tricks saved us, Bea."

"I've never seen a bear stand up like that. Whoa."

"Me neither."

"Is that a good sign to see a bear walking? Or a bad sign?" I ask.

"Mémèr would know," Florence replies.

"I miss her so much."

"And Mom too," Florence says. She reaches over, wraps her arms around me, and squeezes.

"A bear hug." I sigh. "A real bear hug would be pretty scary."

# Part Seven

# *The Huskies and My Big Adventure*

# 33

I sit on my bed with the map in one hand and my rock in the other. Is there anything else I need to do? Everything for my adventure is hidden in a secret spot in the boathouse. Today is the day!

"Nooooo!" Ernest shouts from the kitchen.

I rush down the ladder.

"No, no, no, no, no!" Florence cries.

I run to the kitchen and notice eggshells piled on the counter. They're making eggs for breakfast. Florence and Ernest stand over the pan making faces.

"Oh, Bea! There's a gull in there," Florence says.

"What do you mean? In the egg?" I ask.

"Yes. A little baby gull. We can't eat a baby gull for breakfast," Ernest pouts.

"I cracked the egg in the pan, and a gull popped out," Florence shivers.

"Oh my gosh!" I wince as I look in the pan.

"The last chicken died. Dad thinks a wolf got it. We're running out of food," Florence explains.

"William and Alcide are fishing again. These are all the gull eggs we can find," Ernest says.

"But now with the baby in there, I don't think we can eat any of the eggs," Florence says.

The screen door slaps. "How are those eggs?" Dad asks. "I'm starving. Must be all that dancing last night."

"The eggs are not good," I reply.

"Got a live one, Dad," Ernest says.

Dad walks over to the stove. "Yeah. That happens sometimes. Poor little *bébé*. I'll take it out. We'll have oatmeal then." Dad takes the frying pan outside.

Ernest sits at the table. "When's Mom coming home?" he asks.

Florence grabs a pot and adds some water using the hand pump. "I think the train arrives Tuesday. Dad will row the boat into town to get them. They'll stay a night or two in the house on the Point before coming out to the island."

"They've been gone so long," Ernest says.

"Yeah," Florence says. She opens the cupboard and takes out a bag of oats.

I gather bowls and spoons, setting them on the table. Today is the day. I can hardly believe it. I say it over and over. Today is the day. The sky is clear. Waters are calm. After breakfast, I will sneak to the boathouse and row to Burritts Bay to find the gold. Today. My insides squeal with happiness.

"What's going on with you?" Florence asks.

"What do you mean?" I find the bowl of brown sugar, add a spoon, and put it in the center of the table.

"You're not usually so helpful." Florence looks at me carefully.

I smile. "Just excited that Mom and Mémèr will be home in a few days," I reply. How does she always know when I'm up to something?

"And you're also up to something." Florence makes faces at me. She tries to wink, but it looks like blinking. She remembers I have a treasure map. "Whatever you're doing, I could help," she adds.

"I'm just enjoying the company of my family. Nothing to report here." I smile. There's no way I'm bringing Florence on my adventure today. I need to do this alone, to show them I'm not baby Bea the Bean anymore. To find the gold and to help everyone have a better life.

After breakfast, I'll make a little bundle with snacks. And then, set sail! Well, not sail. Row. But I like the drama of "set sail!" Woo! Today is the day!

# 34

"Batten down the hatches!" I say to Whiskey and Wine as we row away from Gereaux Island. They ride up in the bow of the boat. Their tongues hang out in the wind, and their tails wag. They are excited to leave the island too.

Given how scary it was to meet a bear yesterday, I thought it would be best to bring the huskies with me. I pretend this is a schooner with a mighty sail and the huskies are my crew of sailors.

Wearing my sash around my waist the way cousin Tony showed me, like a voyageur, I row south to Whitefish Channel. I sing all my favorite songs, and then we go west toward the open water of Georgian Bay. *Waaseyaagami-wiikwed.* Shining Waters Bay. The waters live up to their name today, sparkling in the sun. I pause at the end of the channel. Normally, I'm not allowed to row in the open water, but it's the only way to get to Burritts Bay. I'll try to stay close to shore.

My heart pumps as I dip the oars and pull, the boat easing out of familiar waters. Whiskey and Wine bark every time they notice a shoal. I steer the boat carefully, sweating from the effort of keeping us moving.

The sky is blue, but big cumulus clouds move toward us. As long as the wind doesn't pick up and the weather doesn't change, it should be fine. Dip the oars into the water, pull them toward me, swish them through the air. Keep moving clouds. Dip, pull, swish.

When my arms start to ache, I take a deep breath. The mouth to Burritts Bay is up ahead. Dip, pull, swish. The huskies bark. A grouping of shoals on the left pushes us out farther into open water, away from shore. I look at the rolling waves, the dark bay, then Whiskey and Wine. They bark. Well, we've come this far.

Dip, pull, swish. My gear rolls as the waves grow. My bare toes grip the belly of the boat. The huskies move closer to me. The bow of the boat rises as we go into open water without the shelter of the land. Dip, pull, swish.

"We'll row directly into the big waves," I shout over the wind. "If the waves roll up the sides of the boat, we could capsize."

They bark.

Dip, pull, swish. I look over the side of the boat like I've done so many times before. Is the water darker? Deeper? Even though I'm rowing as hard as I can, we make very little progress in the waves. They pull us farther from shore instead of toward Burritts Bay. My arms hurt so much I can't feel them anymore. Dad makes this look so easy.

Dip, pull—splash! A giant wave crashes up over the bow of the boat, soaking me and the huskies. Then another. I clutch the oars with every bit of strength I have left. Dip, pull—splash! Another wave covers the boat. Whiskey and Wine bark madly, shaking like they do after a swim, their paws splashing in the water growing in the boat. When they move the boat becomes even more unsteady.

Dip—splash! A wave knocks an oar out of my hand; it plunges into the deep water, before popping up again and being carried off away from me. Oh no! This isn't good at all. What will I do with only one oar?

"Pépèr! Please help us to Burritts Bay!" I pray. Dip into the water, slice the air. Dip, slice. I use the oar like it's a paddle. First on one side and then the other. We might drown out here. What was I thinking rowing out this far alone? Dip, slice. Dip, slice. Breathe.

The huskies stop barking. They sit in the bow again. The clouds pass to the north, and the waters calm as quickly as they went wild. The huskies and I float gently in the rowboat toward shore as I try to steer it with the one oar I have left.

Once we're in Burritts Bay, I rest the oar inside the boat and let us drift a while. It's safe in the small bay. Although it's wider than Whitefish Channel, the islands on either side provide shelter from the changing winds. No big waves here.

"We haven't seen another human since we left," I tell the huskies.

A gull flies overhead, squawking.

"Sorry about breakfast!" I shout. It likely wasn't her eggs, but you never know. It's best to be in good standing with all the birds and animals. Sometimes they're our only friends.

A fish jumps from the water beside the boat, making a splash when it goes under again. "Oh my! Did you see that?"

Whiskey and Wine bark.

"Maybe they haven't had visitors in a while. Since Tom? What did you think of Tom?"

Bark. Bark.

"Me too. He was so mysterious." I reach into my dress pocket for the map. It's soggy. The waves that soaked us soaked the map. My heart thumps loudly. I open the wet paper carefully. All the words and images are smeared.

"What will we do now? The map is ruined. We only have one oar. My arm muscles are burning from rowing. How will we ever find the gold and get home before dark?"

Whiskey and Wine whimper.

I wish I'd brought the painting with me. I close my eyes. I've looked at the map and the painting so many times, maybe they're printed in my mind. An island with a slippery elm and three white pines. The water low and the shore higher. Then a small birch tree.

I look around Burritts Bay. With one oar I try to guide the boat.

What were those words again? Burnt something. Umber. Cadmium. Cerulean. Sienna. Wait! I've seen the word *umber* before. It was on one of the small paint tubes in Tom's crate of supplies. Maybe these are the names of paints? That might be helpful for an artist, but it's not useful information for an explorer looking for a treasure.

"What now?" I ask Whiskey and Wine.

They say nothing.

# 35

We continue to drift deeper into the quiet bay. The big open water becomes smaller behind me. I scan the shore for a slippery elm and three white pines. Mom says it's called slippery elm because the inner bark is slippery. Sometimes Mom makes tea with the bark when I have a sore throat. It's a large, leafy tree. The outer bark is rough. The branches and leaves are wide near the trunk and then a shape that is narrower near the top.

White pines are more common on the islands. Every island has them. It's amazing how they grow in the small cracks of rock on the islands. They have bundles of needles instead of leaves. The strong winds blow white pines, shaping their branches to look like they are stretching or reaching out. Each one has a different personality. The white pines are more like spirits or friends than trees.

Mom says the rocky islands were formed during an ice age over two million years ago. Some of the layers of rock look like brown sugar and others look like salt and pepper. Each island has unique designs and patterns left by melting glaciers.

Even though the islands look alike at a first glance, the rock formations and the trees will show me the way. I close my eyes again. I imagine every detail of the painting and the map. Twice. Then I open my eyes.

There, right in front of me is the island I've been dreaming of all summer. We floated right to the spot.

"Well look at that. I don't believe it. We found the island!" I shout.

Whiskey and Wine bark in unison.

It isn't easy to steer the boat to the island with one oar. It takes the rest of my energy to get us there. Then I jump over the bow onto the island holding the rope. The huskies jump out too. I look for a rock to tie the boat's rope around and then take a moment to rest on the warm granite. We made it. We're here. Whiskey nuzzles her face in my arm. I swivel so my back is to the water. Look at the slippery elm, three white pines, and the birch. I'm inside the painting. If Tom Thomson were here now and painting this scene, it would include me.

"*Bonjou,* island!!" I shout. "This is now forever known as Huskies' Island." Seems to be a good way to name things, just by saying it is so.

Whiskey and Wine bark. Dad always says they're working dogs first and friends second. I don't think he's right. These huskies are my friends.

I take the rock from Captain Rickley out of my pocket and hold it up to the sun. It sparkles. I cover it with my hand so it's in shadow. It still sparkles.

"See this. We're looking for more of this." I show it to Whiskey and Wine. They smell it. Wine licks it. "Where is the gold? Do you know how to find gold?"

Whiskey and Wine rest their heads down.

"You look like you're ready for a nap. So am I. What if we closed our eyes for just five minutes and then we'll search for the gold. All that rowing tired me out!"

I put my head on Wine's back and fall asleep nestled between the two huskies.

It seems like I'd only closed my eyes for a moment when they open again. My body still aches from rowing. I stretch. Rub the backs of Whiskey and Wine. They open their eyes and yawn.

"Well, let's get looking for the gold."

I look out at the water and see a boat far off in the distance. I wave. *"Bonjou!"*

At a closer look, the boat is empty. Wait. I look over to the spot where I tied the rowboat when we arrived. It's gone.

"Oh no! That's our rowboat!" I cry.

Whiskey and Wine bark.

"That wasn't supposed to happen. Is this really what an adventure is like?" I ask them. "I can't swim over there!" Now we're stranded on the island with no food, no matches, no fishing line. Everything is in the boat. All I have are a soggy map and a rock in my pocket. My dress and my sash.

"What do we do now? How will we ever get home?"

On the shore's edge I yell "help" for a while. My voice echoes across the bay, bouncing off the other islands. It doesn't change the situation. I remember Dad telling me about rescuing boaters before who had SOS messages. I gather sticks and write SOS on the shore. Dad says it means "Save Our Ship." There isn't a code for Save My Rowboat so this will have to do.

The sun is in the west, out over Georgian Bay. This means it's late afternoon or early evening. "Let's find some food."

The huskies and I go into the bush looking for something to eat. I find blueberries. I tap the bush with a stick for snakes and then sit next to it, eating as many blueberries as I can. This will help for today. Tomorrow I may need to eat grasshoppers. Please, someone find me before then.

I swing on some leafy trees to pull the branches down. Then I drag them to the opening near the shore. I need to find a spot to make a shelter to sleep in tonight. Over by the rock where I tied the boat there's a crevice and a bigger rock. I make a shelter using the leafy branches. This way I can keep watch for passing boats. Whiskey and Wine nap in the sun as I build the shelter. They don't seem to be worried about being stranded on a Georgian Bay island.

"We live on an island. This shouldn't be so bad, right?"

The huskies say nothing.

When the shelter is finished, I'm thirsty. I kneel by the bay's edge, scoop up water into my hands, and drink it.

"We're stuck here. Might as well look for gold. This is why we are here." I find a large stick. All the bark is gone, it's been chewed by a beaver. The teeth marks make little grooves in the wood. It's a little bigger than a baseball bat. At school we play baseball every day. It's my favorite sport. I decide to bring that as I walk into the bush. A bear bat. I would never bat a bear, but it helps me feel safer. The best thing to do when you see a bear is to stay silent and still or to make a big noise. I'd use my bear bat to make a lot of noise. I tie my sash around my head.

"Are you coming?"

Whiskey and Wine follow me into the bush. It doesn't look that much different here from our island. Trees, moss, rock. I don't see anything sparkling. Where's the gold? As we pass blueberry bushes, I put more blueberries in my pocket for later. I pick up every rock I find and look for the sparkle. I lie on my belly and try to see it in the rock formations of the island. No gold.

A crow flies and lands on the top of a spruce tree.

"Crow is that you?"

*"Caw, caw."*

"It's me. Bea-the-Bean." Then I'm crying, using the ends of the sash around my head to wipe my eyes. I've planned all summer for this adventure. Everything keeps going wrong.

*"Caw."*

"Say Flor-ence," I whisper.

Crow flies away. I don't think it's her. That's just a normal crow.

I walk back to my shelter. Still no signs of boats or people. As the sun goes down, it disappears behind the trees. The sky doesn't light up in different colors. Sunset here is quieter and less dramatic than on our island. Maybe it's because the islands and trees block the horizon line. I miss our island. There's no breeze here either. The mosquitoes start to bite. This is a disaster.

"This might be our life now." I sigh. The huskies disappear in the woods for a bit. Hunting probably. Sometimes on our island they chase bunnies, and Mom says they want to eat them.

I'm usually horrified, but today with no other options, it makes more sense. The huskies won't eat many of the blueberries I offer. They need to eat something.

"An island is really quiet without family," I tell Whiskey and Wine when they return.

I thought for sure there would be gold on this island. How could I get it so wrong? I'm so tired I fall asleep before dark, snuggling with the huskies.

# 36

I wake up in the dark from Whiskey and Wine barking hysterically.

"Bea! Bernice!" Dad shouts.

"Dad? Dad! I'm over here!" A lantern floats across the bay. The huskies continuously bark and run circles on the island. When it gets closer, I see the boat and Dad, William, and Alcide too.

"Thank goodness! You're safe!" Dad shouts.

"We were so scared!" Alcide shouts.

It's hard to hear them over the dogs.

"Where's your boat?" William asks.

"It floated over there." I point across the small bay.

"Good thing you brought the huskies with you!" Alcide says.

"We heard them barking, and they led us to you!" William adds.

"Do you have anything else with you?" Dad asks.

"Just Whiskey and Wine. Everything else is in the boat." I walk over to where I made an SOS sign, kicking the sticks to clear it. I didn't need that after all.

Dad's big rowboat moves closer to shore. I can see their faces in the glow of the lantern.

"How did you find me in the dark?" I ask.

"Florence thought you might be in Burritts Bay. Something about a treasure?" Dad says.

"I'm sorry! I'm sorry!" I cry. My shoulders shake up and down. It's hard to catch my breath. "It wasn't supposed to happen like this."

"All that matters now is you're safe." Dad jumps out of the boat to the island and lifts me up in his arms. "We can talk about the rest in the morning."

"I wanted an adventure," I whisper. "I wanted to find the gold! To get money to help our family. There is so much that we need. It could solve all our problems."

"You certainly had an adventure, though I don't know what you mean about finding gold and solving our problems," Dad says. We climb into the boat. The huskies happily jump in too.

Alcide taps me on the shoulder as I pass by. William hugs me when I sit next to him on the bench.

"Florence and Ernest are waiting for you at the lighthouse," William says.

"Just in case you came home while we were out looking for you," Alcide adds.

"Why do you have a sash on your head?" William asks.

I pull the sash down and wrap it around my waist.

"Now let's get that little rowboat," Dad says. He dips the oars into the water and pulls.

"How did you lose your boat?" William asks.

"It's a long story," I reply. Wait until they hear I lost my oar too.

"You rowed all this way?" William asks.

"It wasn't that far," I reply.

"It's far, Bea. Really far," William says.

Alcide holds the oil lantern out over the bow of the boat. It reflects across the water. "There it is!" he shouts.

Dad rows up beside it. He attaches a rope to a hook on the bow for towing.

"Now we go home," Dad says. "Looks like you're missing an oar."

"It floated away," I whisper.

It's dark and quiet all the way home. It's hard to stay awake. How can Dad row in the dark? I can barely see anything. My eyes droop with exhaustion. The moon is only a sliver tonight. Stars twinkle. I can see the Milky Way and Orion's Belt. I even see a shooting star.

As we leave Burritts Bay, I realize I forgot my rock with the gold from Captain Rickley on the island. It doesn't seem to matter now. How can something that was so important in the morning be less important by night? I'm just so happy to be safe with my dad and my brothers.

Dad expertly navigates the two boats through the open water of Georgian Bay and around the shoals back to Whitefish Channel. I see the glow from the light tower welcoming us home, showing us the way to our island in the dark. As we pull into the boathouse, dawn breaks and the sky begins to turn from black to gray.

William and Alcide bring the huskies back to their pen.

"Let's get some sleep," Dad says. He lifts me up in his arms and carries me home.

# 37

"Wake up, Bea," Dad says.

I pretend I'm sleeping.

"You can't stay in bed all day. Get dressed and meet me on the turret," he says. His footsteps get quieter. The rungs of the ladder make a faint ring as he climbs to the tower.

How can I face them after making so many mistakes yesterday? I'm embarrassed they had to rescue me. What kind of adventurer needs to be rescued? Searching for gold gave me a purpose, a way to give to my family. Something to think about. Something to do. How will I go back to a boring old life?

"Bernice! Let's go!" Dad shouts.

I sit up slowly in bed. The room is empty. The sun shines brightly in my window. I get dressed and put my hair in a ribbon, a sad, low ponytail. I pull the sheet up to the pillow and smooth it. Anything to delay talking to Dad.

Someone put the Tom Thomson painting from the boathouse in our room, leaning on the floor near my bed. I turn it over to face the wall. On the back, it has cursive writing like on the map. Four words. Two words look like they start with T and two words look like they start with B. Maybe T is for Tom? And maybe the B-words are for Burritts Bay? I'll have to ask Florence. Why didn't I look at the back of the painting before? I stared at it so many times but only from the front. Just another mistake to add to the list. Another teaching about how important it is to look at things from all sides before acting.

I watch the floor as I mope to the ladder. My arms still sore from all the rowing yesterday, I climb to the turret sluggishly. Dad stands on the outer balcony, his hands on the rails, staring toward Burritts Bay. Outside, I pick a spot a few feet away from him. I sit on the balcony floor with my back against the tower. My legs and toes poke out under the railing into the air.

Dad doesn't turn to look at me. He continues to gaze out at the expanse of islands and channels. "I want to tell you a story, Bernice. I wasn't much older than you when I was in Whitefish Channel exploring. On one of the islands, I found a couple of arrowheads. They were made of stone and used for hunting long ago. During those days I spent more time with our cousins at Henvey Inlet First Nation."

I pull my legs in and cross them. Then I shift a little to watch him speak.

Dad continues, "My dad often told stories about the Robinson-Huron Treaty. It was an agreement made between the government and the First Nations people in 1850. It decided things about rights to the land and fishing and hunting. Dad's Pépèr helped with some of the translating for the Anishinaabeg when it was being created. Dad's mémèr helped too."

I move in a little closer.

From here I can see Ernest opening the pen, letting Whiskey and Wine out, giving them fresh water and some cooked fish. The huskies drink and eat quickly before running off. I send them love with my eyes. Wine keeps running, but Whiskey pauses, turns, and looks at me. Bark! Then off into the bush with Wine.

Dad smiles, then stares out at the islands as if they are helping him to remember his story. "A treaty is an agreement. Treaties support a good relationship. Treaties can show a way to share land and resources."

"Do we have a treaty?"

"We are all treaty people. Treaties belong to everyone. But they need to be honored. As more settlers moved from overseas, more things were being taken from the land to build communities: lumber, minerals, fish, beavers."

"Like all the trees here?" I think about the logs that travel by water from the islands, down the river, to the sawmills.

"Like our trees. All this land is the traditional territory of our Anishinaabe cousins. They cared for it for thousands of years. We owe them a great gratitude."

"I love our cousins." I wish we saw them more often.

"Me too. And since I was your age, I've felt that our cousins have been treated unfairly."

"How?"

Dad twists around to point north. "The islands on the north shore that you visited are on Henvey Inlet First Nations land."

"Is our island Henvey Inlet too?"

"This island belongs to the government. So does the land to the south, even Burritts Bay."

"Land belongs to the government?" I find all of this very confusing. "Doesn't land just belong to the bears and crows and snakes? Aren't we sharing the land?"

"That's what we believe, Bea. The land and the waters here will always be Indigenous lands and waters. And we also know that others have a different way of looking at the land. To some land means money, not relationship. Pépèr was upset because a lot of land was taken from our cousins."

"Did we have land taken too?"

"Our home was Drummond Island, but after our community moved to Penetanguishene, it was never the same. Life became harder for each generation. Our family was told we were nothing after the death of Louis Riel. And First Nations people we loved were told they had to live in reservations instead of roaming the land and waters as they'd always done. We were told where to hunt and fish. There were rules about who belonged and who didn't. It was unfair. Rights and freedoms we always had were taken away. Land was taken away."

"Why don't our Henvey Inlet cousins go to my school?" I ask. I just realized I never saw them there.

"I don't know, Bea. I wasn't allowed to go to school when I was your age." Dad releases a big breath.

"This is really sad."

"Pépèr was so angry, and it made me angry too. And we were angry because there was always land and jobs and fish enough for the settlers. It's like a different set of strict rules is given to those of us who are Indigenous."

Crow lands on the railing near Dad. Below, Florence is hanging the wash. Ernest and Alcide are fishing by the boathouse.

William is whittling something in the shade. I can see my whole family from the tower. Everyone but Mom and Mémèr. I can't wait until they are home from Toronto. I miss them.

"When I found the arrowheads out on an island, I thought they would be a nice gift for the cousins at Henvey Inlet. I could give them back something that belonged to their history. It felt right to give them something because so much had been taken. Like you, I got into my little rowboat and went into the open waters on a nice day. My journey took me north. Once I got past Cunningham's I followed the channel toward Key River. I just kept rowing. I didn't know where they lived or how to get there yet. I was too young and hadn't paid enough attention when Dad took us. I thought I might see some cousins on the shore or recognize one of their homes. But it was like they had vanished. Erased. No one was visible from the main channels. I kept rowing north. Then it was sunset."

"Did you bring your dogs?" I whisper. In the tower we are so high up I can see the far side of the island too, past the bush and trees, Whiskey and Wine sniffing around by the water's edge.

"Didn't even think to bring huskies. It was just me and the rowboat with two little old stone arrowheads."

"How did you get home?"

"Well, it all worked out in the end. Just before nightfall I ran into Old Man Rickley," Dad replies.

"Is Captain Rickley that old?" I stand up next to Dad at the railing and lean into him.

"How do you know Captain Rickley?" Dad asks.

"It's a long story," I reply. It seems ages since my visit to town and meeting with Captain Rickley.

"It was his grandfather. He was out fishing. Old Man Rickley insisted on leading me home in the dark," Dad explains. He puts his arm around me.

"Was your family mad?"

"There was so much going on that day because my oldest sister, Adelaide, was about to marry Tommy Bushey. No one had noticed I was gone until they saw Old Man Rickley and me show up at the campfire." Dad smiles.

"Did your cousins ever get the arrowheads?"

"A few days after the wedding, Dad took me out to Henvey Inlet to visit. I gave them the arrowheads then. They said the story of my adventure was the real gift. And then over the years, the visits were less and less. We all got so busy surviving. That's my story, Bea. Sometimes we do things to help others without realizing we may need some help too. We need to work together."

"Thanks for sharing this story, Dad." I close my eyes briefly to print it in my mind.

"I think you have a story to share with me." Dad sits on the turret's balcony with his back to the tower, and I join him.

# Part Eight

## *Finding the Family Gold*

# 38

"Do you remember Tom? The artist in the painted canoe who slept in the living room?" I ask.

It feels special to sit with Dad on the turret. I've helped Dad plenty of times when he's tended the light. Mostly, he does all the work and I chat. When he isn't filling up the kerosene, he's trimming the wicks, winding the clockworks, or cleaning the lenses. Florence and I clean the tower windows as part of our chores each week. They've always got moths stuck to them. We stand on a stool and scrape at them with a scraper tool. It's not much bigger than my hand. The tool has a wooden handle with a piece of thin, flat metal on the other end. We soak the window first with soapy water, carefully scrape the dead moths off with the tool, wipe the window again with soapy water, and then dry the window with some rags.

Dad sits with me quietly. He doesn't answer the question right away. The stillness makes me nervous, so I start to talk.

"When I was listening at the door to the kitchen the morning Tom Thomson left, I thought you were talking about real gold," I whisper. "Gold coins, treasure." As it comes out of my mouth, I realize I built a treasure hunt on something I heard while spying.

"A talented man. He painted the islands and the bay so beautifully, captured the spirit of this place. Pure gold," Dad replies. "A different kind of gold." His legs stretch out way longer than the balcony. He takes off his hat and rubs his head. It's warm sitting in the sun, and the tower blocks the breeze from getting to us.

"That's where it starts. I wanted to find the gold to help everyone." I tell Dad everything: about Mémèr finding the map, me meeting Captain Rickley and learning about the gold in the rock, and then me talking to Tony about maps and how to get to Burritts Bay.

"Florence helped me read the cursive writing on the map, even though those strange words didn't really help me, and then yesterday I rowed to Burritts Bay. I thought for sure there would be gold that I could bring back to help pay for so many things," I explain.

Dad doesn't say anything. My chest tightens. My palms and forehead sweat. How much trouble am I in for spying on Tom and then rowing a long way into the open water alone? And losing an oar! I had told myself that I was looking for gold so I could help everyone, but as I tell the whole story to Dad, I see that it was mostly about having an adventure. It was all about me. My imagination carried me away, and I made a big mess.

"Do you see all those islands out there, Bea?" Dad moves his arm to show me.

I pour my heart out to him and he wants to show me islands? "Of course I see the islands. I look at them every single day, Dad."

Dad smiles. "There's gold in every single one of them."

I stand up and look over the rail. "I've never seen gold on those islands. I looked all over the island in Burritts Bay and found none. Our island doesn't have any either."

"It's not what it seems. The gold is in the veins of the granite, a little piece here and a little piece there. It's not really enough to mine, although some find a way. Mica mining is more profitable around here. But the gold, Bea, it's out there. You were right. It's part of all the land here."

"Even our island?" I ask.

"I'll show you." Dad leads us into the tower and down the ladder, through the house, and outside to the granite rock the lighthouse sits upon.

Florence joins us as we pass the kitchen. She passes me a piece of bannock. "I thought you might be hungry," she says. Over the last couple of weeks, she's become an incredible cook. Maybe even a better cook than Mom, but I'll never say that out loud.

Ernest collects kindling nearby. He places some sticks on a bigger pile, waves, and then runs over.

As we follow Dad, I eat the bannock in two bites. "Thanks, Florence. Just what I needed." I could eat a whole pan of her bannock.

Dad walks us to the eastern tip of the island. He crouches and gently runs his hand over the top of the granite. "Feel this," he says.

We put our hands on the rock too.

"It's warm," Ernest says.

"Energy. You can feel it," Dad says.

"From the gold?" I ask.

Florence rolls her eyes. "You can't feel gold like that, Bea."

"It's one of the oldest rocks in the world. You can see the lines of quartz there. Some white, some pink. But look here. I found this when I was a kid." Dad points to a crevice in the rock.

I lean in, cupping my hands over the rock. "It sparkles! Gold!" I shout.

"Let me see!" Ernest pushes me out of the way.

"Gold, right here on our island," Dad says.

"How do we take it out?" Ernest asks.

Florence moves in for a turn. "It's pretty!" she squeals.

"Is there more?" I ask. Then I move in for another look.

Dad sits back on the rock, watching us take turns looking at the small vein of gold in our island.

"If I use a chisel, it might damage it," Ernest says. "Explosives?"

"We'll leave it for now. But you can visit it whenever you want. Sometimes it's best to appreciate things as they are, leave them where they are. Show your kids the gold one day. We don't always have to take something just because it's there," Dad explains.

"Imagine. Gold on our island all this time," Florence says.

"We have so much to appreciate today. War has just been declared in Europe. We don't really know what it means for us here. Yet we share a moment like this together with the land, grateful for what we have right now. *La famiy sé nawt vra awr.* Our gold is really our family," Dad says.

I give him a hug and cuddle against him for a minute like when I was little. Dad kisses the top of my head.

"When you decide to go exploring, tell us about it, and bring your sister or one of your brothers," Dad says. "And no open water. Stick to the channels."

"I promise," I reply.

"Is the war coming here?" Ernest asks.

"It's on the other side of the world right now, but some men in town are getting ready to go help the British," Dad explains.

"Can I help?" Ernest asks.

"Not for a few years. Your brothers are too young too. We need you all with us right now," Dad says. He rubs Ernest's hair.

"Will you have to leave?" Florence asks.

"The government sent a notice out saying that lighthouse keepers are needed to support the war by keeping the lights shining and watching the waters to guide ships. More ships than usual will be coming through to connect with trains. Supplies for troops. I'll be staying right here with you."

# 39

A few days ago, Dad rowed to town and learned at the post office by telegraph that Mom and Mémèr are finally coming home! I can't believe they've been gone almost all summer. We've worked hard to make the lighthouse look nice for their return. The boys caught a feast of whitefish. Alcide already has the fire going for the party. The fiddles rest near the woodpile, and Mémèr's rocking chair is outside waiting for her. Ernest and I used pieces of moss and stones to spell the word "*Binvnu*," welcome, on the shore, so they'll see it from the water.

I sit outside on lookout.

Crow flies from the east and announces they're on their way. "*Caw. Caw.* Bea-the-Bean. Flor-ence," she says.

"Ernest! They're coming!" I shout.

"William, Alcide, Florence, it's time!" Ernest shouts.

Our whole family will finally be together. To celebrate, Florence even made little cups of wildflowers to put in every room. She added Queen Anne's lace, daisies, black-eyed Susans, and some water lilies.

We run to the dock to watch them arrive. Soon we see the boat.

"*Bonjou!*" I shout.

"*Binvnu!* Welcome home!" Ernest shouts.

"We missed you!" Florence adds.

Mom waves.

As the boat floats into the dock, Mémèr says, "Who was here? What did I miss?"

"You! You were missed," Florence shouts.

We laugh. She's still Mémèr.

"*Mémèr, on a bin dé zistwèr a trakonté.* We have so many stories to tell you," I say. She looks like she shrank. How could Mémèr be getting smaller?

"Oh! You've all gotten so big! I've missed you!" Mom says. There's something different about her. I can't figure it out.

"You're wearing spectacles?" Alcide says.

"Yes, I can finally see," she replies. "I went to a doctor in Toronto. I never dreamed I would be able to get spectacles. And how nice to be able to look at all of you." Mom gets out of the boat quickly, giving us each a long hug. The gold wire curls around her ears. Another wire rests on her nose so two glass pieces are at her eyes. They are wonderful. I've never seen spectacles up this close before. I can't wait to try them on later.

William and Dad help Mémèr out of the boat. Mémèr does a slow little spin. "See. Good as new."

"Careful, Maamaa," Dad says. "You need to take it easy."

"We're going to have a feast!" Ernest says.

"How wonderful! Lead the way!" Mom replies.

Ernest grabs Mom's hand and pulls her toward the house.

Alcide and I walk on either side of Mémèr, holding her. She squeezes my hand. I squeeze her hand back.

"You ready to finish that beading lesson?" Mémèr asks.

"Really? You still want to teach me after having to go to the hospital. I'm so excited! I didn't think you would ever bead again," I reply.

We lead Mom and Mémèr to the house like it's their first time here. Ernest gives them a tour, proudly showing off how well we kept everything while they were gone. William and Alcide cook the fish on the fire. Dad sits on a log and offers them advice. Florence flutters about offering everyone homemade blueberry tea.

"It has blueberries, obviously. Some wintergreen, sumac, and honey," she explains.

I watch Mom and Mémèr like they're strangers. What will I talk with them about first? So much has happened since they went to Toronto. My heart overfills with being so close to them that I can't even say a word.

# 40

One day shortly after they're home, Mom asks Florence and me to join her in gathering some plants.

"This is the best time of year to harvest. Then we will dry the plants to use in the winter," Mom explains. She passes us each a basket. "It was far too long to be away. We still have so much to catch up on. Let's go to the south side of the island. We need some sumac, St. John's wort, wintergreen, sweetgrass, yarrow, and some blue asters if they're blooming. It might be too soon." Mom leads us over the rolling path of granite and moss through the trees, around the snake bushes, and across the island.

Mom was born in Byng Inlet. She learned all about gathering plants from her mother. Her parents moved to Byng Inlet from Quebec when logging started. Her dad, Grandpa Michaud, was a carpenter, and he helped to build one of the mills in town.

"Sumac!" Florence shouts.

"Clip the clusters of berries away from the trees," Mom says.

Before I cut the stem with the berries, I crush some of them between my fingers, staining them red. The velvety texture feels so nice. Then I lick my fingers. "What is that taste?" I ask.

"They're tart, Bea. Don't eat them yet. They're not sweet like blueberries." Mom smiles.

"There's some wintergreen here too." Florence points to the ground and a patch of wintergreen growing among the moss.

"Just what I need to get rid of that tart taste! Ew." I pull a wintergreen leaf and nibble on it. "Ah! Refreshing!"

"All right, Bea. Let's start putting some in the basket," Mom says.

We quietly add berries and clippings of plants to our baskets. Everything we need is in one area of the island. Mom knew just where to lead us.

"We're lucky to have so much growing on our island," Mom says.

I wonder if this is an example of the other kind of gold that Dad talked about. We do have a lot of wonderful things growing all around us.

We sit for a few moments by the shore in the shade of a slippery elm. There are snake bushes around us. Mom says they're juniper bushes, but I always call them snake bushes. We are in the company of white pines, spruces, and birches. The granite rolls, curves, and dips around the plants, bushes, and trees. As it gets closer to the water, the moss thins until patches of bare rock glimmer in the sun next to sparkly waters.

"I'm proud of you girls. I want you to have every freedom," Mom says. "I heard they're adding grades seven and eight to the school. I didn't get a fancy education like you. My mom taught me how to read and write at home. I want a better life for you, so if you'd like to go back to school when it reopens after the summer, Florence, you can."

"Really? Yes! Of course! I love school! This is better than I could have imagined!!" Florence does a jig for us on the rock. I jump up and join her.

"More school!" We cheer.

Mom leans back and watches us, her eyes glistening like the water on a sunny day.

"You were gone a long time," Florence says.

"Did you see motor cars?" I ask.

"And electricity," Mom says.

# 41

After a few hours we walk back to the lighthouse. Mom had returned earlier to leave us to finish harvesting. We put our baskets on the step.

"Time to bake," Florence says. "I'll come back for the baskets shortly."

Inside the lighthouse, I find Mémèr in the living room. I sit on the floor next to her rocking chair.

"I missed you, *ma pchi*. I bet you have some good stories to share. What about that treasure map? Did you ever follow it?" Mémèr taps my head.

"I followed the map, but I didn't find any treasure. Dad says there's more gold right here, but it lives inside other rocks. It isn't easy finding gold with a map or when it's right where you live. You have to really pay attention," I share.

"That's because there's no treasure greater than your family, *ma pchi*." Mémèr reaches into her pocket, then covers something with her hands. "Your mom took me to the Eaton's store the day before we came home. The store was so much bigger than Cornish's! You can buy so many things and even things you don't need. I bought you a gift."

She opens her hands. It's a small toy mouse.

"I thought you would like a mousey." She runs the mouse up over my shoulders and head. Then she leaves it there sitting on my head.

"Oh, Mémèr, you're so silly!" Balancing the mouse on my head I move around the room while Mémèr rocks in her chair and laughs like old times.

"Thank you, Bernice, *ma pchi*. Your laugh is my favorite gift," she says. "Oh, and look! Your mémèr is famous. They printed an article about me in the Toronto newspaper. Ha!"

Mémèr pulls a folded piece of paper from her other pocket. She passes me a clipping:

> Mrs. Lamondin was sent to Toronto General Hospital for removal of a needle she swallowed while sewing.

"Mémèr, I'm so glad they helped you!"

# 42

Just before sunset, Dad calls us to the rock in front of the lighthouse. We are on the eastern tip near the vein of granite with the gold.

"It's been a big day. I'm sure you'll remember today for the rest of your lives," he says.

Mémèr and Mom link arms like sisters. Ernest smiles proudly as he carries his small canoe from the shore. He rests it nearby in a curve of granite. Alcide sits on a large rock with his fiddle. He was on his way up the tower to play on the turret when Dad called. William runs from the boathouse, clutching my copy of *Treasure Island* by Robert Louis Stevenson. Florence swings a pocket watch Mémèr brought her from the city. It catches the sunlight and twinkles.

Dad scoops me up and puts me on his shoulders. I'm wearing my sash over my right shoulder, across my body, and tied at my hip. I put it on after dinner to show I'm still an adventurer. But I learned some things about asking for help from others before setting out, and I've finally learned where to find the real treasure. I can see it all around me. Wearing the sash says I'm proud.

"I want you to remember this." Dad gestures to the rock, the water, and the sky. "This is who we are and where we come from. We may change the story, but it doesn't change us. Whether it's Georgian Bay or *Waaseyaagami-wiikwed* or Shining Waters Bay, it lives on just the same. The bay knows itself and its stories. We are still the same people too, no matter our name, and we live on just the same. No one can take our stories. You get to keep those no matter what happens. Be proud of your stories. Your treasure, your gold."

"One day it will be safe to share them. And then, let your stories shine like the light at the top of that tower for all to see," Mémèr whispers.

We watch the sky change colors for a while. Then Alcide picks up his fiddle. *Su nawt rawch, nawt il, nawt chenou on chant pi on dans ansanb.* We sing and dance together on our rock, our island, our home.

# *THE HISTORY OF THE REAL BERNICE AND HER FAMILY*

*This book was inspired by the author's family history.*

1650s–1850s: **The fur trade.** Many of Bernice's great-grandfathers were voyageurs who worked for Ezekiel Solomon, Bernice's ancestor, or the Northwest Trading Company. Her great-grandmothers were Ojibway, Saulteaux, and Métis.

1761: **Ezekiel Solomon** arrived in Michilimackinac and became a highly successful trader who wintered in Montreal. He opened new trade routes into what is now northwestern Ontario. In 1781, he faced financial losses, and the family moved to Mackinac Island. He was the first Jewish settler in what is now Michigan. He was Bernice's great-great-great-grandfather.

1759–1855: **Chief Kechewaishke** (also known as Chief Buffalo) signed numerous treaties in what is now the United States. He was an Ojibway leader. He was possibly Bernice's great-grandfather.

1812: **The War of 1812.** Bernice's ancestors lived in Mackinac. Métis soldiers (including her family line) fought alongside the British and helped to defeat the French.

1815: **Mackinac Island** became part of the United States. The family moved to Drummond Island with the British troops and seventy-five other Métis families. From 1821 to 1825, the family lived on St. Joseph Island as part of a peacetime garrison, to notify the First Nation people of the area of the British. William Solomon (Bernice's great-great-grandfather) worked as an interpreter.

1828: **Drummond Island** became part of the United States. The family was one of the last to migrate to **Penetanguishene** in 1829. Louie Solomon (Bernice's great-grand-uncle) left behind an oral account of their journey.

1850: **The Robinson-Huron Treaty** was entered into agreement. It includes Henvey Inlet First Nation and Magnetawan First Nation that are mentioned in this story. Bernice's great-grandfather, William Solomon, was one of the interpreters.

1867: **Canadian Confederation** joins Nova Scotia, New Brunswick, and the United Canadas (Ontario and Quebec).

1869: **The town of Byng Inlet, Ontario**, on the Magnetawan River was established and became one of the largest lumber towns in Canada at this time.

1873: **Gereaux Island Lighthouse.** Bernice's grandparents moved from Penetanguishene to Byng Inlet. Her grandfather, Joseph Normandin, became the first lighthouse keeper.

1876: **The Indian Act** came into force in Canada, restricting Indigenous rights.

1885: **Louis Riel**, leader of the Métis people, was charged with high treason and executed. He had led two resistance movements to advocate for Métis rights.

1898: **The *Northern Belle***, a steamship, caught fire and drowned on the Magnetawan River, near Byng Inlet. No lives were lost. The wreck became popular with divers.

1908: **The Canadian Pacific Railway (CPR)** between Toronto and Sudbury opened on June 15, with stations in Byng Inlet North (Britt) and Byng Inlet. The introduction of steam locomotives had a big impact on the town. **Byng Inlet North** was renamed to **Dunlop** after a local rail engineer.

1910: "**Mrs. Lamondin** was sent to Toronto's General Hospital for removal of a pin she swallowed while sewing." Friday, June 3. *Toronto Daily Star*. (Likely Bernice's mother or grandmother. This timeline was adjusted for the story.)

1911: **Coal dock** opened. Ships arrived in Dunlop (Byng Inlet North) with coal to be loaded onto train cars. The coal docks operated until 1956. As the logging industry faded, the coal industry created jobs.

1914: **Tom Thomson** visited Georgian Bay. He may have visited the lighthouse in June. On the back of the sketch for his painting *Byng Inlet*, it says Gereaux Island Lighthouse. William was four years old and Alcide was six years old. On July 28, **World War I** began. **French River Village** (a nearby logging center) was torn down.

1921: **Bernice Lamondin**, who inspired this story, was born in Dunlop (Byng Inlet North). (To connect with the Tom Thomson visit, this timeline was adjusted for the story.)

1927: **Dunlop was renamed to Britt**, after Thomas Britt, superintendent of the Canadian Pacific Railway's fuel depot in Montreal. The Graves Bigwood and Lumber Company closed its lumber mill, and most people moved away from the area. Bernice's family stayed and continues to have roots there.

1939: **Highway 69** extended to Britt. By 1956, it would extend to Sudbury. Bernice and her family did not have access to motor vehicles until the late 1940s.

1946: **Louis Lamondin** (Bernice's dad) retired as lighthouse keeper of Gereaux Island. He continued to live in Britt.

1952: **Hydro power** came to Britt, Byng Inlet, and surrounding area on January 16. Bernice and her family in Britt used kerosene, coal, and wood until then.

1956: **Oil ships** began to use the Byng Inlet harbor. Oil was stored in oil tank farms (and then distributed by truck or used by the trains). Bernice married an American sailor, Art Armstrong. He became the captain of the *Martha Allen* from Indiana (an oil ship) that often docked in Britt.

To learn more about the history of the area:

William A. Campbell, *Northeastern Georgian Bay and Its People* (W.A. Campbell, 1983).

Fred Holmes, *The History of Byng Inlet and Its Shoreline Communities* (F. Holmes, 2004).

John Macfie, *Parry Sound Logging Days* (Boston Mills Press, 2003).

## LETTER FROM THE AUTHOR

Dear readers,

My great-aunt Bernice and our Métis family story inspired this book. She was one of my favorite people. Starting when I was around eight years old, I followed her around with my note-book, asking her to tell me stories about life at Gereaux Island Lighthouse.

This book is fiction, yet some of the stories she told are included: her dad making them candy on the island, the swing in the boathouse, brushing her teeth with ash, her whole family working so hard, and the joy when the family gathered to sing and dance.

Her siblings were really named Alcide, William (my grandpa), Florence, and Ernest. The family changed their name from Normandin to Lamondin to hide their Métis story. They were afraid after Louis Riel died. Our family always knew they were Indigenous but were not allowed to talk about it until recently.

Bernice's dad, Louis Lamondin, is verified by the Métis Nation of Ontario in the Ontario Métis Root Ancestors project. He is from the Solomon and Berger/Beaudoin family lines.

Captain Rickley was a real person from Britt during that time, although in real life I don't know if my family knew him. To help build a character, several details are imagined (including his glass eye). However, according to local history, he was known for eating rattlesnake meat in soup. Now, the massasauga rattler is threatened and protected, so no one should be eating it.

I was lucky to grow up with lots of music, shore lunches, and large family gatherings on the islands. Over the generations, my ancestors have worked hard, lived on the water, and always valued family most of all. I wanted to write this book to capture the spirit of my great-aunt Bernice and the distinct life they lived at the lighthouse. My parents live in Britt, less than a mile by water from the lighthouse today.

Sincerely,
Jessica Outram

Gereaux Island Lighthouse, early 1900s (family photo)

The real Louis Lamondin (Dad in the story), William, Alcide, and Cecilia (Mom in the story), in 1912 (family photo)

Gereaux Island Lighthouse (shared with permission from Steve Wohleber), c. 1921

# *ACKNOWLEDGMENTS*

Special thanks to my family, cousins, aunts, and uncles for sharing your memories with me. I was lucky to speak to several descendants of Uncle Alcide (we call him Uncle Nye), Grandpa William, Aunt Florence, and Uncle Ernest. Aunt Bernice did not have children, but she was very close with her many nieces and nephews.

Thank you to Sandy Barron for sharing pictures and stories too. Sandy's father, Joseph G. Barron, was lighthouse keeper when Great-Grandpa Louis retired in 1946. Sandy lived with her family at Gereaux Island Lighthouse until 1966.

Thank you to Gillian Rodgerson from Second Story Press for your generous encouragement from the very beginning of this project. Thank you to Chandra Wohleber for your editing excellence. It meant so much to work with you.

Thank you to *Waaseyaagami-wiikwed.* Shining Waters Bay. Georgian Bay.